THE APOCALYPSE OF MORGAN TURNER

Cover design: Debbie Geltner
Layout: WildElement.ca
Printed and bound in Canada.

Library and Archives Canada Cataloguing in Publication

Quist, Jennifer, author
        The apocalypse of Morgan Turner / Jennifer Quist.

Issued also in electronic formats.

ISBN 978-1-988130-62-0 (softcover).--ISBN 978-1-988130-63-7 (HTML).--ISBN 978-1-988130-64-4 (Kindle).--ISBN 978-1-988130-65-1 (PDF)
        I. Title.
PS8633.U588A85 2018   C813'.6   C2017-906563-7
                                                           C2017-906564-5

The publisher is grateful for the support of the Canada Council for the Arts, of the Canada Book Fund and of the Société de développement des entreprises culturelles (SODEC) for its publishing program.

Linda Leith Publishing
Montreal
www.lindaleith.com

THE APOCALYPSE OF MORGAN TURNER

a novel

JENNIFER QUIST

DEDICATION

In 1985, my modest father balked at bringing the
"World's Greatest Dad" mug I gave him into the office.

But enough is enough, and this book is dedicated
to Lloyd Allan MacKenzie, World's Greatest Dad.

1

What everyone knows is that Morgan's sister—the victim, slain Edmonton woman, Tricia Turner—is dead. Everyone has seen the footage on the newscasts, the headlines, the blurry colour pictures on the front pages of *Sun* newspapers, all of them showing the heavy blue tarp draped over winter-dry alfalfa, the place where Tricia's bones and hair and clothes were found. A needle in a hayfield—that's what she was, in the end.

"Female remains located near Innisfail, Alberta, in May of this year have been positively identified as those of missing person, Tricia Turner, of the city of Edmonton. Incidents surrounding Ms. Turner's death have been deemed to be of a criminal nature. Twenty-four-year-old Brett Finnemore, also of the city of Edmonton, will be arraigned at the Court of Queen's Bench on charges of second degree murder and offering an indignity to a dead body. Ms. Turner and Mr. Finnemore were known to each other. These events were not random and there is currently no threat to public safety."

A police communications officer read the statement into a microphone at a press conference. Positively identified—Morgan still doesn't know why it was written that way. "Positive" usually means someone is happy about something, or at least relieved. Everyone said the family must be relieved now Tricia was dead in a box instead of dead in a field. No, of course they meant positive as in being perfectly sure about it. Morgan asked her brother Tod what it would have meant if female remains had been negatively identified as their older sister's. What he said was, "Morgo—what the hell?"

What no one knows is the truth of why Tricia was killed. It matters enough to be decided by strangers, with a public trial of the man who killed her.

Today, on the couch in their mother's living room, Tod is watching for the news, spearing Cheezies out of a plastic bag with a fork to keep the greasy orange powder from his fingers and pants. On someone else, it might be dainty. He eats, Morgan wipes at crumbs in the kitchen. They continue the wait that began the night something happened at Tricia's sketchy walkup apartment building, something bad between her and the person she loved. It is one of those stories. Tricia can't tell it for herself, but she doesn't have to. Stories like hers are like old horror movies, the kind people call classics, as if they know them well and the movies are part of them even though all that most people remember are highlight reels, one or two famous scenes. Everyone knows the shower scene from *Psycho,* recognizes it shot by shot. Lesser known are the film's other scenes—the ones about money and secretarial work and bad boyfriends. No one knows that *Psycho* anymore.

Over time, the entire movie has contracted to not much more than close shots of wet skin and threads of chocolate sauce in running water, swirling down a drain in black and white.

"News is coming on," Tod calls to Morgan from the couch. He means the noontime broadcast where their mother will be appearing. Their mother is dimly famous in the city, a figure from local news clips, dressed in black and grey, squinting in daylight. She will be standing on the steps of the bleak, brown courthouse downtown. Someone once said the entire building is supposed to be a Brutalist rendition of the scales of justice. Morgan still hasn't found anyone who can tell her how to see it that way.

For the news people, Morgan and Tod's mother is a sound-bite machine for outrage at the criminal justice system. They film her near the sign that reads "Law Courts," spelled out in black metal letters that leech their colour into the concrete behind them in wet weather. On television, the news directors print Morgan's mother's full name beside their station logo, tucked into the bottom of the screen.

"Sheila Turner, Mother of Victim."

It took time for Sheila and Marc—her ex-husband, Morgan, Tod, and Tricia's father—to settle into their television personae. They began like people who win the lottery and are brought to face news cameras still in their stretch pants and ball caps and kitchen sink dye-jobs. The viewing public deserves to hear everyone talk about their fortunes, and bad fortune is still a fortune. Whenever Morgan sees her parents on the news, the colour of their eyes isn't right, and their faces are covered in tiny pock-marks and excess flesh.

Sheila will be alone on television today, looking less like the lottery folks and more like the professionals from the court's Victims' Services office—scarves, and fancy earrings ticking backward and forward as she speaks, metronomes of indignation. She has learned the language of protesters and picket signs, scoffing at "justice" like it's the Ogopogo.

Strictly speaking, it wasn't Tricia who put Sheila on TV, in the newspaper, making her famous. It was that guy, that Finnemore. The Turners are not the kind of family to ask or to tell each other about their romances, so none of them knows why Tricia was dating him. "Dating" makes it sound like he bought her milkshakes and held her hand, the both of them strolling under gently drifting choke-cherry blossoms. The truth is Finnemore never bought her anything, never took her anywhere—not until the end, when he bent her body into a hockey equipment bag, zipped it, and tipped it over the railing of a third-floor balcony into a shopping cart on the lawn below.

Tod spears the Cheezies, the TV news moves through the morning's tragedies—layoffs at a mill, a truck rolled over on the Henday Freeway. Morgan stands in her mother's kitchen arranging glasses in the dishwasher, clearing away the breakfast mess now that it's noon and she can't stand the reek of cold coffee and toast crusts anymore. Both of the surviving Turner siblings know what they will see on today's news report. There will be B-roll of the crime scene—the blue tarp in the brown field.

There will be the photo screen-captured from Finnemore's online dating profile, one with his shirt hiked up, his bare abdomen flexed and reflected in a speckled bathroom mirror. Sheila will speak to the cameras, repeating her lines about her "daughter's life sentence."

Morgan kicks the dishwasher closed and watches the television screen from behind Tod. He crumples the empty plastic bag between his palms. "We have got to get Mom a thesaurus before she goes down there again. There's must be another way for her to say 'slaughtered.'"

There are many words Sheila could have spoken but has never said to the news people. In all of Sheila's speeches, in all that has happened, one word in particular remains unsaid. Morgan has been waiting for it from the very beginning, listening to hear Sheila say the word "evil." She will not hear it today.

This is the first time Sheila has been broadcast from the courthouse without any of her children standing behind her on the concrete steps. Maybe it's too soon to have sent her alone. Pointless as it is, maybe one of them should have gone with her this time, every time.

Tod knows and says, "There was nothing to see down there today, eh Morgo? I know it, you know it, Mom knows it. Everyone knows it—even those microphones and cameras, they know it. They just came in case it turned out there's nothing much to report in the city today but that fact that Tricia is still dead. Breaking news!" he bawls. "Deceased Edmonton woman still every bit as deceased as she was last year."

It is true that nothing happened to Brett Finnemore at the courthouse today. The paralegal from the prosecutor's office called Sheila last week to explain precisely what kind of nothing the Turner family should expect. Today's hearing was a brief appearance to set a date for something that won't happen for months. Setting it over, setting it over, they're always setting it over. But Sheila once swore, in the presence of the news people, that every time Finnemore came to court he would have to face her. For each court date, she books time off from her nursing unit at the hospital, drives downtown, pays for parking, passes through the courthouse security check point, climbs the stairs to a courtroom, and faces him—a heavily medicated prisoner in leg irons, standing in a box, looking at no one.

The news clip has already ended. They get shorter each time they're aired. Sheila was barely onscreen. Now there is nothing but a commercial starring a happy, happy lady from a mattress store. She used to brag about having enough mattresses to build a stack that would reach to the moon. She doesn't say that anymore. Something must have gone wrong. The commercial isn't worth watching again and Morgan is looking at the crown of Tod's head instead. The colour and texture of his scalp is visible through sparse black bristles. He keeps his hair shorn, the best treatment anyone knows for a little baldness being a lot of baldness.

"That's that," Tod says. He shifts and the couch creaks and lists beneath his weight like a canoe about to capsize. Since they were kids, he has more than grown up. He has grown huge. He rolls and heaves himself to standing without exerting quite enough force to flip the couch backwards, on top of his sister. He's leaving.

"Got to get to work, Morgo."

Tod's workplace is called a factory. It is actually an abattoir, off in an industrial park where no one but truck drivers and its own employees can see it. He is paid union wages to scald hog carcasses until the hair sloughs off the hides. Morgan has never seen him do it, and he acts like powerful people don't want him talking about it. She is left imagining him in a massive rubber apron, a hook in each hand, his scalp slicked with steam from the scalder and his own sweat. She has asked him about it—what it smells and sounds like—asked him so many times, in so many ways that he has raised both of his hands, then his voice, and said, "What is with you, Morgo? Give it a rest. You're creeping me out." His work has stayed a grisly fairy tale. Morgan has watched for traces of hogs' blood on him. She has never seen any, but she is fairly certain she has smelled it.

Tod doesn't have to report for work for hours, not until three o'clock this afternoon. He told Morgan so this morning and then forgot she already knew, goofed and used work as an excuse to leave the house, to leave her. He remembers as he grips the cold knob on the front door, but it's too late to take the fib back now. He pauses in the open doorway, vents his breath into the late October air, steaming as if he has grown not just huge but hard as tin, a giant, pot-bellied clockwork man. "See ya," is what he says as the door closes behind him.

Something about Morgan's presence corrupts his clockwork, something soft and gummy, silent and smothering. She knows it, but knowing she's doing it is not the same as knowing how to stop. Tod hates it, hates himself for it. He has tried to suggest ways to lighten her presence, make it easier to abide. He's done it subtly, as if none of it matters. "Hey Morgo, your voice would be cuter if you'd crank the pitch up a little—make it brighter. You know."

He has also tried, "How come you never wear any make-up, Morgo? It wouldn't kill you, would it? A bit of eye shadow or blush or whatever the hell it is the rest of them do to themselves."

"The rest of them"—this is Tricia. She was made up every day since she was eleven years old. She always kept a boyfriend too, even after she should have outgrown boys. Her preference was for young handsome guys with wax in their hair and expensive tattoos. Maybe if Tod had one more sister, a third one, she would be Goldilocks—not too cold, not too hot, just right.

Tod drives away, toward the abattoir. He will arrive hours early for his shift, park his car in the sunlight, set its heater to low, and open the book he has been driving around with all year—the one about how everything we can't see is bad, and it's smart, noble, and good to be nasty to people who believe in something. He will try again to read it.

Morgan is left with nothing to look at inside a house that has been too familiar for too long. She stands at the living room window. The snow in the front yard is new, pricked by tips of grass buried alive. She is feeling for the nearly invisible power button on the top edge of the television—black plastic on black plastic. The light and chatter in the room disappear as she shuts it off. The picture window beside the TV credenza is clouded on both sides of its pane by a dusty white cataract. She sits behind it. Through the haze, she will stare out at the street like a thoughtful, beautiful leading lady in one of the old movies Tricia used to have to watch as homework when she was in college. Morgan will sit behind the glass as if time lapse cinematography is pulling shadows across her face. She will sit still—scrawny butt against the hard edge of the credenza—until her mother comes home from the courthouse. Through the window, from the street, Sheila will arrive home to see her un-slaughtered daughter.

As it happens, Morgan is gone when Sheila returns to the house. By then, Morgan has walked out to the avenue and boarded a bus bound for the restaurant where she works. She is a wreck on the cash register, useless, but they bring her in every day just as lunch ends to clean up the mess. The bus's rattling onboard heater was set too high, mounted too close to Morgan's seat, blew the smell of the fast food uniform in her bag all over the place.

There is no one sitting in the living room window when Sheila comes home, walking through the screen door bracing her temples between her thumbs, exhausted, angry. Court appearances like today's, they take all morning to start but they end quickly. The judge leaves first. A courthouse sheriff leads Finnemore through a side door, sends him back to the remand centre where he is kept waiting for his trial. After the formal proceedings and the moments with the media, Sheila and her children end their court days meeting with the prosecution team in a small office for debriefing.

In the office, Sheila doesn't have to gag back words like "abuse" and "travesty." She can tell the prosecutor and the paralegal all the things that might have been contempt of court for her to say before a judge. She can point and wave, give orders and instructions, remind them they cannot know what Finnemore has done to her family.

"Yes. I see. But I'm sorry," the prosecutor has answered, "I'm sorry, but I'm not your lawyer, Ms. Turner."

His claim to being sorry is like a sign in a Wal-Mart parking lot saying the company "regrets" it can't be responsible for damages to vehicles—polite, insincere, aggressive.

The first time the prosecutor declared he was not the family's lawyer, Sheila stopped, stunned. He went on. "We appreciate your input in Mr. Finnemore's matter. We take it very seriously. We don't pretend to be able to comprehend your grief and we want to give you all the respect and support we can. Your rights as a victim of crime are guaranteed under the law. But, all that said, I can't take legal instructions from you."

Sheila shook off the stun, leaned hard against the back of her chair. "Not our lawyer. So, you're working for Finnemore?"

"No, no—"

"But you're not working for Tricia?"

"That's right."

"Then whose lawyer are you?" she said. "The police's lawyer?"

The prosecutor shook his head but only slightly. "I am nobody's lawyer."

He is terrible, dispassionate as a shark or an earthquake, a force that cannot notice something as small and noisy as Mother of Victim.

No, that's not it.

The prosecutor is a man—like the man in the long, black robe in another one of Tricia's old movies, one they watched as part of her school assignments. She and Morgan read the dialogue from subtitles while the actors spoke their lines in English so muddled Morgan couldn't quite understand it. Tricia laughed at her and shoved her into the arm of the couch. The language was actually Swedish. The man in black was supposed to be death itself, a word the actors pronounced differently but not unrecognizably: *döden*. Even if it had been dubbed in Chinese the sisters wouldn't have needed subtitles to know who he was. He looked out of the screen at them—black eyes sunk into sockets in his face—and he said, "*Jag är ovetande.*"

I am unknowing.

The man prosecuting Finnemore for killing Tricia sounded the same when he spoke to Sheila. "I am unknowing" or "I am nobody's lawyer"—it's the same.

At least the prosecution team was stable—the same lawyer, the same paralegal at every meeting, phone call, court date. Finnemore, on the other hand, kept firing his lawyers, disrupting the proceedings, powering them down and then up again, trying to reset them and send everything back to the start. It's a frightening move in a legal system where his right to a speedy trial is protected even if it results is no trial at all, his charges stayed, unanswered. The prosecutor explained that getting a stay of proceedings is *usually* not something that can be done simply by stalling with fired lawyers. The uncertainty of his "usually" was too much. Sheila couldn't wait for the legal people to sort it out. She told them she was going to make her own formal complaint to the politicians who run the Department of Justice—not merely a stern email but something monumental, like a candlelight vigil at the big sandstone provincial capitol building on the edge of the North Saskatchewan River. It was spoken as a threat but the prosecution team didn't seem scared. They might have been grateful, relieved for her to be taking the fight outside—to a place where they might get some help.

Sheila needed the Finnemore prosecution to become personal as badly as the prosecutor needed to keep it from getting personal. He moves with Sheila through the emotions of the legal proceedings like partners locked in a dance—a waltz where Sheila is leading, stepping forward while the prosecutor steps always back and away. Once when she went to take a mighty, crashing step toward him during an after-court meeting, he raised one finger, stood up from the table, and answered his phone.

The Turners were left alone with the paralegal, Morgan watching the prosecutor's back through the sidelight window in the office wall as he spoke into his phone in the hallway. He dresses either in his long, black grim reaper barrister robes or in dark suits, usually the kind with two rows of buttons on the front—double-breasted, they call it, though Morgan thinks it's a creepy name. They're the sorts of suits that make fat men look fatter and skinny men look skinnier. The prosecutor is neither. He is barely tall and his hair is a bit slick, pushed up and away from a face full of bone—eyebrows, cheekbones, jaw-lines.

"I don't know why he thinks he can treat us this way," Sheila said.

Unofficially, part of the job of the paralegal abandoned in the office with the Turners is to smooth things over when a prosecutor is acting like an ass. She said, "Sorry about this. We've been expecting an urgent phone call about a live police situation all morning. It's unfortunate but the demands of our workload make our schedules a bit—hectic."

"Well *I* didn't do anything to deserve to be left waiting like this," Sheila said. She waved at Morgan. "Neither did my daughters."

"No, of course not."

"Why does he seem so unorganized all the time?" Sheila went on. "He's supposed to be some homicide hot-shot but some days he seems more like distracted summer student help. I mean, come on—look at him. How old is he? How much experience—"

"Yes, people are often surprised at how busy we are. But Mr. Lund is very good at what he does. There's no one better," the paralegal said, adding before Sheila could speak again, "and you can't fire him. Mr. Lund was correct in saying he is not your lawyer."

Sheila let out her breath, loud and exasperated and infusing the little room with the smell of her morning coffee. "Then who does he work for? Someone tell me, once and for all. Is it something lofty and abstract like the people of Canada? Because I am the people of Canada."

The paralegal smiled. "It would be something like that down in the States. But up here, he works for the Crown—Queen Elizabeth II."

Some people are spooked by the sound of their own voices in strange places. Morgan is among them. She spoke up anyway, repeated the unanswered question her mother had asked. Maybe she did it for Tricia—her older sister with a penchant for young men. There, in the debriefing office, Morgan asked the paralegal the prosecutor's age.

The paralegal startled, blinked. "Who? Finnemore? How old is Brett Finnemore? I'd have to look it up to be sure but I think he's twenty-six now."

Sheila twitched in her chair. "No, not Finnemore. How old is the prosecutor—that Mr. Lund?"

The door opened. The prosecutor was back, waving his cell phone like it was an explanation. He didn't sit—made no move toward the empty seat he had left at the head of the table. "I had to take it, sorry."

The paralegal was first to realize the meeting was over, stacking file folders that hadn't been opened, pulling them toward herself.

"Hey, Coleen," the prosecutor said to her. "Sorry, but we need to get that arrest warrant extended, right now before the flight leaves the airport."

It was theatre meant for the Turners. Coleen played her part. "Whoa, urgent."

"I'm afraid so."

Someone in trouble was at the airport, heading for the border, and without the prosecutor's approval the police would not have the power they needed to detain him. It was sensitive information and he could only hint at it enough to justify, but not explain, why he had to leave the Turners so gracelessly. Yes, they had lost a daughter and sister. But she was already gone, not like the man in the secure airport boarding lounge, flipping through the offerings of the free Wi-Fi, about to feel a strange hand on his shoulder. The Turners' old, dead tragedy was about to be rolled over as the system moved on to something new—something that might be salvaged.

"So the next hearing will be in October—October 28th at ten o'clock in the morning," Coleen told Sheila. "If you come up with any new questions before then, please give us a call."

"That's it?" Sheila said. "One phone call comes in and we're kicked out?"

"I really am sorry. But you're welcome to keep using this room as long as you need to," Coleen said. "Nobody is getting kicked out."

Sheila smirked. "Nobody again, eh?"

Coleen stood in the office doorway, a strong brown

box full of Brett Finnemore's homicide file in her arms. She smiled again. "Hang in there. It's frustrating, but it can't go on forever."

Still seated at the table, Morgan bit at the cuticle of her index finger.

Sheila swatted at her. "For God's sake, Morgan…like a deer in a trap."

2

"Where are you?"

This is Gillian Lund's favourite text to receive. It means, "Enough. I am coming to see you now."

"Where are you?"

This is her least favourite text to send. It means, "You are supposed to be here by now. But you're not."

This is the text she has just sent to her younger brother, Joshua Lund. His work is intense, decorous, impossible to interrupt. He is a prosecutor who needs to mute the ringer on his phone when he's in court. Between his muted ringer, tying up the line calling out, or mashing his phone into airplane mode without meaning to, the idea that Josh can be reached through twenty-first century wireless communication technology is essentially a sham. Gillian is trying to meet him today anyway, driving all the way across the river from the university. She is parked in the loading zone at the foot of a shiny, curvy government office building that houses the province's prosecution services. With his phone muted, Josh is unreachable on the sixth floor, behind silvery glass she can hardly look at in the noon sunlight. Gillian waits in her cold little car, idling almost noiselessly on the street where city buses drop people off to report to their probation officers on the building's lower floors.

Now her phone is ringing. It's Josh, crackling from an elevator. "Sorry, Gigi, I'm coming down right now. I was in court all morning. The Finnemore file—you remember. Yeah, his new lawyer wanted another adjournment. More delay but at least it's not our fault and it shouldn't count as time against us..."

Gillian can see him now, on the sidewalk, the wind lifting the hem of the dark wool coat she and Leanne, his wife, found on sale at that weird outlet store. Gillian remembers following Leanne through the men's section, pushing a shopping cart full of nieces, each of them red and sticky with the lollipops Auntie Gigi had given them in a store full of clean, cloth merchandise.

"Hey," Josh says, bending into the front seat of his sister's car.

"I've got a seminar starting in fifty minutes," is what Gillian says instead of "hello."

"Sorry. Like I said, I was stupidly busy—"

"What I'm saying is we need to eat somewhere fast, no table service—somewhere kind of gross. We need a place with French fries and probably lots of kids."

"Sure. That's my scene anyway." He squints at her across the front seat. "What's with your face?"

"Shut it, Josh."

"No, it looks different than usual, like, better."

She punches his arm. "I actually pencilled in my

eyebrows this morning." She bats his fingers away as they move to poke her brow. She's laughing. "Can you not be cool about anything? Just leave it."

Josh sits back. "Honestly, I don't think I've ever seen you accept a compliment." He snickers for just a moment before launching into a long, procedural story about a tricky bail application—something from the real, painful grind of police work and prosecutions. When his stories aren't shocking, sensational to the point of absurdity, they are technical and tedious. Josh doesn't always know the difference anymore. He is still talking about bail as Gillian wheels into the parking lot of a fast food restaurant, its plate glass windows covered in translucent cutouts of cartoon characters.

Inside, Josh makes a spectacle of himself at the counter, ordering French fries without any salt. He is sent away to wait for a new batch the staff will have to hand-deliver to their table.

Gillian laughs at him. "Joshua, if you'd ever worked in a restaurant yourself, you wouldn't act this way."

As they eat, she asks him about the file that had tied up his phone all morning while he appeared in court. Everyone wants to know about the Finnemore file—the homicide where some maniac bashed his girlfriend's head in, dropped her off a third-floor balcony, then drove the body down to Innisfail, to the usual dumping grounds— the open fields between the secondary highways and range roads, the distance at which murderers fleeing crime scenes in Edmonton realize they're getting too close to Calgary, panic, turn off the main highway, and roll their stiff, sad cargo out onto the prairie. They do it like they were all issued the same defective brain—as if evil is cranked out on a filthy assembly line, rote, boring, and broken by design. In fiction, criminals are masterminds, manipulators with ingenious plans of execution and evasion. In life, the criminal element is one sad, stupid mess after another.

"How are they?" Gillian asks. "How's the victim's family holding up? They would have been at the courthouse this morning."

"Yeah, but it was the mother all by herself today," Josh says. "By herself and doing as badly as ever. She's mad about the court date getting set over so far into the new year. Of course she is, poor lady. Like I said, new lawyer, new adjournments. Oh, and the new lawyer on the file—it's Dean Orenchuk."

Gillian groans. "No, he's terrible."

Josh rants on and on, all the way to the end of what members of the public, like his sister, can know about Brett Finnemore's homicide trial. When he finishes, he is drained—his spine bowed, his head bent low over the greasy tabletop. "Sorry, Gigi. You must be sick of hearing it."

Gillian sits up straighter on her plastic seat. "No, actually. That's exactly why I asked—why I wanted to see you today. The idea I have for my dissertation is really coming together. But I need to use you as a consultant."

Josh raises his head. "You need me to consult on a literature thesis?"

"Yes. We're making a study of legal writing as a form of incidental found literature. And it will take me forever and be boring as frick if I don't narrow it down to the transcripts of contemporary criminal trials." She puts one hand over her heart. "I need you as my guide, my inspiration, my muse, Joshua—the one to save me from writing a thesis that's just another book report for the university to throw on the pile."

"Muse—knock it off."

"Come on, I'd be crazy to spend three years reading criminal court transcripts without using you as a resource. And I won't forget to put your name in the acknowledgments."

"So I won't have to write anything?"

"Heck, no. Please, no. The writing is mine. All I want from you are tips on which trials are important and worth looking into—like a reading list. I want to watch you from afar at the courthouse, listen to you talk about work, like we're doing right now. That's all I want."

"Sure, I'll help," he says, picking at Gillian's uneaten fully salted fries. "I need to work on being helpful—more charitable and kind. I get rushed and single-minded at work and I'm not always a nice person."

Gillian scoffs. "You're nice enough. Once you turn your phone back on, you're always good to old Gigi."

"That's because you're not unreasonable and you don't make me crazy."

Josh does know how to pay a compliment, and it's got nothing to do with eyebrow grooming. Gillian overacts

21

her acceptance of it with a grand bowing of her head. It's a mistake, sending the room slanting and swirling.

"Woo!" she sings.

Josh's hands clamp on either side of her head. "Uh-oh. Are you spinnin' again?"

She is sitting still while something at the centre of her head tells her she has been flung in circles, sending her reeling with a ridiculous medical problem. It's not even a problem, more of a glitch, known as benign paroxysmal positional vertigo. Particles have been set adrift in the fluid inside the semi-circular canals of Gillian's inner ear—the organs meant to steady her sense of equilibrium, her body's understanding of its position in space. "Crystals" is what the doctor calls the particles. Gillian imagines tiny, sparkling, cursed amulets lost inside her head. They tumble, colliding with the sensory neurons in her ears when she turns her head too fast or too far. She is dizzy, not in the way people with low blood sugar or a bad flu use the word "dizzy" to describe light-headed wooziness. She is dizzy in the true sense of the word—spinning, unable to move for fear of falling, arms extended, teetering into walls, everything she sees strewn through her field of vision, forms dragged into streaks of colour.

Josh tightens his hold on her head, as if it will help. "Did it stop yet?"

She strains to move between his hands but he doesn't let go.

"*Deng yi xia,*" he says, an artifact of the Chinese he used to speak when he was a very young man living as a missionary in Taiwan. The words mean, "Please wait a bit." Right now, he uses them to ask Gillian to stay still and let the dizziness pass completely, not to be embarrassed but to pause and recover. *Deng yi xia*—Gillian uses the phrase herself sometimes, pronouncing the Chinese wrong, accidentally saying something that sounds more like the Chinese words for sand and lanterns. It's been too long since he lived his life in Chinese himself, and Josh doesn't notice she's saying it wrong. Gillian has seen her nieces responding to these words as if they're plain English when Josh uses them to ask his daughters to be patient. To the little girls, the clumsy Chinese of their father is part of their native language.

Gillian would have waited longer, but Josh lets go of her head when someone comes to stand beside them—a stranger, quietly sliding Josh's tray of dirty napkins and empty wrappers off their table, like a pick-pocket or a magician. She is a woman dressed in the restaurant's uniform—ponytail and a hat, stiff, pleated black pants, and an oversized golf shirt with a floppy, worn out collar that rolls into a tube instead of folding into a crease.

None of this would be strange if Josh didn't seem to know her. He looks the woman in the face and says, "Hey, you work here?"

She nods, not looking anywhere near his face.

He is standing up, piling the rest of their lunch debris onto Gillian's tray for the uniformed lady, as if he owes her something—as if he's sorry. "Thanks," he says as she carries their garbage away.

23

Gillian nods at the woman's back. "A friend from work?"

This is their code for identifying someone who has been caught up in the machine of the justice system while Josh stands at the crank and turns the gears. Sometimes, he meets them in the course of mundane family life. Tragedy doesn't excuse people from having to shop or stand in line or work at counters. Victims, witnesses, accused people are all around, some of them trying to talk to Josh on what they hope are normal terms. They might say, "Done in court for the day?" or make some other casual but knowing remark about his not-at-all secret crime-fighting identity. They speak to him like people who have learned a few words in a foreign language, experimenting on a native speaker—their own borrowed fragment of a language they don't actually speak, their own versions of something like Gillian's *deng yi xia*. Josh responds with the same terse mix of surprise, disorientation, and suspicion that native speakers use in their replies.

"Yeah, she's from work alright."

Gillian nods again. "Someone I've heard about?"

"Oh definitely." He won't say the name out loud, so she leans one ear toward his face, pointing at it so he will whisper. He shifts beneath the moulded shoulders of his outlet overcoat. "The Finnemore victim—that's her sister. That's Morgan Turner."

Josh and Gillian watch from across the dining room as Morgan bends over a dustpan. Her lank pony tail is the right length to catch in her collar, teasing itself into frizz

24

and hard, tiny knots. She won't look back at the Lund siblings, but her shoulders are pulled up, crowding her ears, the posture of an ad hoc amateur actor in a local commercial told to go about her usual business as if there's always a camera crew at her workplace.

Gillian repeats the name in her own whisper. "Morgan Turner."

This girl—her sister was murdered and abandoned by a handsome young maniac. Hardly anyone has lost a loved one the way Morgan has lost her sister. And still, there is no badge of tragedy about her. She is a fixture in this trashy restaurant, clearing tables, shuffling garbage from one place to another. Morgan Turner—she could be anybody.

Morgan's hands are shaking, damp with sweat, as she pulls a bulging bag of garbage out of a bin in the restaurant's dining room and fights to tie its sticky ends into a square knot. There is a slow leak of flat brown pop dripping from one of its corners, leaving trails on the floor. She will be the one to have to mop it. Right now, it doesn't matter.

She has seen one of them—one of the court-people outside the courthouse, nobody's lawyer, the lead prosecutor of Finnemore's trial himself. If this was a television show, she would have seen him somewhere more glamorous than this restaurant—across the counter at a coat check in a concert hall, or while properly waiting a fully-set table in a nice hotel. But real life is dirty and embarrassing and she saw him here, in her cheap fast food restaurant during the cleanup of the lunch rush.

The lady eating with him might be his wife. If their story was a television show—a long plot arc about people solving crimes—this wife would be written out of the script by the end of the second season. Morgan is not catty—not at all. The imminent vanishing of the wife is not a wish, just something she knows. After a few appearances, the wife character is always eliminated. It justifies and glorifies the rest of the story. Her departure doesn't have to be bloody. She can die naturally, though it's harder to arrange in contemporary settings where childbirth is no longer fatal. Having the wife killed is better anyway—more dramatic, good for triggering revenge. Or, without violence, she can come to accept that life with her crime-fighter is one of constant low-grade betrayal—late nights, missed events, unreturned phone calls. The crime-fighter will do his best but she will leave knowing he cares more for the greater good than he does for her. The writers send her off in a way they hope will make it hard for anyone to blame or hate her. Actors ham away at grief for an episode, but everyone on the other side of the screen is happy to see the wife go. There is promise in it.

Morgan doesn't know the real story, where the woman at the restaurant is the prosecutor's sister and his wife is busy with her own matters. Real stories, though dirty and embarrassing, don't come with narrative debts characters need to repay—no dramatic promises to keep. Joshua Lund's wife, Leanne, has a bachelor's degree in music, four bony little daughters, and sells fitness shakes through her social media feed. She doesn't know or care much about television crime dramas. Josh won't watch them. It's for the best, spares everyone the ranting and eye rolling.

"Oh—great. They just breached the bad guy's charter rights. Well, you'd better let him go home now that this confession is useless in court. They've got nothing. It's a disaster. Who wrote this? Who turned this on? Who's got the remote?"

The Lund siblings stand to leave Morgan's restaurant without revealing their story. Gillian pinches Josh's sleeve between her fingers, points out a smear of ketchup on the wool. He licks the corner of a napkin and uses it to blot himself clean. And then they are gone.

Morgan hefts the dripping garbage bag over her shoulder. She carries it through the backdoor, into the alleyway, past a steel vat of black, exhausted cooking oil. The huge metal lid of the dumpster is as heavy as it looks. Morgan edges it open and pitches the bag of garbage over the side. It's light and crinkles into place—plastic and paper and melting ice cubes. She doesn't regret her missed opportunity to rifle through it to find and keep the straw the prosecutor used. She's not crazy, doesn't want his DNA. She's just interested. It's interesting. The prosecutor's appearance at the restaurant feels like something Morgan should report—like a sasquatch sighting. Instead of saying anything she lets the metal dumpster lid drop, banging and ringing through the alleyway like a great steel gong.

The restaurant's back door has no handle on its outside

surface. She has left it propped open, the humid, fragrant restaurant air rushing out of the building. Assistant shift supervisor Vincenta stops in the doorway, her head turned to call out in non-English to someone in the kitchen as she pulls the door closed. "Non-English" is Morgan's name for the language most of her co-workers speak. She once thought it was Spanish. It's not. She'd ruled it out after Tod found her reading a beginners' Spanish phrasebook she had bought at the thrift store for a dollar.

"Planning on going partying in Mexico, Morgo?" he'd asked.

Of course not. She was just hoping to figure out what everyone at work is talking about. When the restaurant is dead and they start speaking Spanish to each other.

Tod had snorted. "Spanish? Sheesh, Morgo. I've seen your co-workers and they're not from Spain. Try the Philippines."

Morgan had kept reading the phrasebook anyway. She has been meaning to look up the real name for the Filipino language but she never thinks of it when she's anywhere but at work.

She lets out a little cry in the alley behind the restaurant as Vincenta is about to slam the door closed.

Vincenta laughs, apologizing. "Morgan! Hurry, hurry," she says. "It's cold, and you're missing Enrique's cake."

Enrique is the daytime shift supervisor. Everyone knows it. The fabric of his work shirt is different from the rest of the crew's—a light poly-cotton shirt with buttons all the way down the front. Even the customers can tell he's in charge. He is not content to run the restaurant forever, and today is his last day of work here. He has fought through the paperwork needed to change the terms of his foreign worker's visa and he can now take an industrial job—one where he can make a better wage. His new job is at Daisyvale, a chicken processing plant in the same part of town as Tod Turner's hog factory. The rest of the lunchtime crew is laughing, talking in loud, fast non-English. They add enough English for Morgan to be able to tell they are joking about their undying loyalty to Enrique, promising to follow him to the factory, standing side by side with him slaughtering feathery lizards, everyone chalky with uric acid.

Vincenta takes both of Morgan's hands and swings them as if she's about to start a dance. "Don't forget this one. Our girl Morgan is coming too!"

The cake is gone, and Morgan mops the floor, dumps the gritty grey wash water into the gritty grey gravel in the alleyway. She signs out on the timesheet and stands in the cold, between the open-air ashtrays on the patio in front of the restaurant, waiting for Sheila to take her home. Sheila wouldn't come late on an ordinary day, but today is a court day and Morgan expects very little.

It's dark when Tod comes for her, dispatched by Sheila, rushed during the break in his shift. He is cranking down the car windows as they leave the restaurant's parking lot.

"Morgo, I'm not letting you in the car anymore unless

29

you either put that uniform in the wash or torch it."

She inhales her own cold French fry stench, tells him her job sucks.

"Yup."

She looks out the car window, waiting before she asks if he thinks they'd hire her at his factory.

"At Freibergs? Sheesh, Morgo, why'd you want to work there? It's a slaughterhouse. You know what that means, right? It's regulated and sanitary but it's a horror movie, all night and all day. It's a horror movie where you can see the directors and stagehands walking around, moving the scenery, and pushing the actors through their paces. Only there are no special effects. The blood's not ketchup. The hogs can't act. They don't pretend to die and we don't pretend to kill."

She knows.

"Look, Morgan, we can't all live in a horror movie. I do. Tricia did too. Someone gets to stay out of it. That's you. Just—just keep wiping trays in the restaurant. Make sure the ketchup pump runs smoothly, okay? That's enough."

3

Overdue notices for Tricia's last library book arrive in the mailbox on Sheila's front step from time to time. They are the final evidence anyone has of Tricia's whereabouts before she went home to her apartment to be killed. The library is a strange whereabouts for her, unexpected. Tricia was bright enough but never library-bound bookish. What she went there for might not have been books but refuge. In cold-weather Edmonton, where finding shelter indoors on an ordinary winter day can mean life or death, public libraries are havens for all sorts of people who can't go home. Classes and statuses mix—organic linen tote bags set on dubiously stained upholstery, tiger mothers and security guards ignoring each other during story time, aspiring writers in community meeting rooms interrupted by apologetic homeless men who've already been chased out of the mall too many times.

Maybe Tricia spent her last days alive as one of the people hiding in the library, too scared to go where Brent Finnemore would know to find her, too embarrassed to let anyone else know. No one can say for certain why Tricia was there, but she had a brand-new library card and used it to check out a graphic novel version of Dante's *Inferno*. Morgan looked it up, the last book Tricia read. It's the first part of a trilogy. There's a final book on heaven and a middle one about a Catholic place called *Purgatorio*. In the twenty-first century, the book on hell is the only one anyone reads. Of course, the library was missing the copy of *Inferno* Tricia borrowed. Morgan had to read it as a jacked ebook instead. It's a horror story even older than *Psycho* or that Swedish film she and Tricia had watched together. It diagrams all the ways we will need to be punished after we die for the evil that we did, the evil that we were.

Morgan asked Tod about it. "*Dante's Inferno?* It's a video game—all full of nipples and big hairy butts. It's not for you, Morgo."

Morgan read *Inferno* alone, without comment or discussion, secretly, on an old laptop computer almost too hot to touch a few minutes after being switched on. She read it in her bedroom, the one next to Tod's, across the hallway from her mother's. In it, sins weren't what people did but who they were—their titles, surnames, species. The book's suicides and liars were tragic enough, but the fate she wanted to know most urgently was that of thieves— people who take things they can't bring back. It's bad. It's snakes—a pit of snakes and thieves, all of them naked and tangled. Snakes coiled around bare hands, wound over and under hips and thighs—snakes biting and burning, forever and ever.

Looking for Tricia Turner's missing library book was

not a major concern of the forensic police investigation. But then, there wasn't much about the unfolding of the forensics that went the way the Turners expected. Real forensics would be bad television, terrible storytelling. Real forensics utterly failed to construct a scene-by-scene re-enactment, a cogent narrative of Tricia's killing like the ones played out on true crime television. The best the police could do was find clues to refute or support the version of events given by Finnemore himself—a version the prosecutor said was deliberately, craftily erratic. Still, Finnemore's confession was taken as a preliminary map, sending investigators looking for proof of his violence all over the ruins of Tricia's remains.

Once female remains had been found near Innisfail, the police matched DNA from them to a spitty Q-tip swabbed from the inside of Morgan's cheek. An anthropologist and a bunch of graduate students from the university were engaged to look at the bones. In addition to the head injury, they found moderate, non-fatal damage all over the body. Her arms, ribs, the occipital, parietal, and temporal plates of her cranium confirmed Finnemore's account of her being bashed on the head, and dropped from a moderately high place. This is how Finnemore confessed it—all in the passive voice, a confession without a culprit. Joshua Lund did not fail to notice. He would bring every issue the judge would allow, even these grammatical ones, to the jury's attention at the trial. Finnemore's defence lawyers claimed he was crazy, so mentally disturbed he couldn't be held responsible for what happened to Tricia, yet Finnemore himself had already been canny enough to include excuses for himself in the police interview room in fine, narrative detail.

There was only one element of Brett Finnemore's confession that had not been found replicated in the forensic record of Tricia's skeleton. It didn't need to be found there in order for Finnemore's story to be true, but the fact that the evidence was missing supported the prosecution's theory of what happened. There was no evidence that Tricia was ever stabbed through her left ear. In his confession, Finnemore told a police detective that he jammed a single takeout chopstick into Tricia's ear—the left ear, the sinister one where a demon lived, speaking messages directly to her brain, controlling her, telling her Brett Finnemore had to die by her hand. He claimed she was going to kill him, and soon. The evil voices in the sinister ear were what he was defending himself against the night Tricia, as he first phrased it, "passed away."

To keep Tricia's demon from screaming up the apartment building after he stabbed it, Finnemore hit her hard in the back of the head with a heavy ceramic lamp—one Sheila had donated to her when Tricia first moved out, a dusty-rose lacquered relic of the 1980s. When she was quiet—demon exorcized, skull pulverized—and her legs and arms were still supple, Finnemore folded her into the brand-new hockey equipment bag she had bought for him at an end-of-season sale. Instead of dragging the bag down the hallway past the neighbours' closed doors, he waited until late at night, bided his time cleaning up broken ceramic shards, dusty-rose dust, mopping up blood with paper towels and pre-moistened anti-bacterial wipes. Near two o'clock in the morning, when no one was outside in the street to notice, he hoisted the hockey bag over the railing of Tricia's third floor balcony, dropping it into a stolen shopping cart he'd pushed to the side of the building. The story broken into Tricia's bones said that the landing was rough, her body falling on the cart more than into it.

The drop worked well enough, though, and he used the shopping cart to wheel Tricia's body to her own car. He jammed the hockey bag into the trunk, drove her to an all-night drive-thru window to get himself an extra-large coffee. Then, like any fugitive in his right mind, he stopped at his apartment to pick up his tool belt and passport, emptied all the cash from his bank account, and left the city heading the only direction most people will travel from Edmonton: south.

The police were already looking for him when Finnemore was arrested for starting a fight at an oilfield jobsite in Saskatchewan—not a regular gentleman roughneck's punch-up but a brawl. He was howling and brandishing a scrap of rebar, jabbing like it was a rapier, swinging it like a club at other men's heads.

According to the prosecution, Finnemore's confession—its demons and chopsticks, its talk of the sinister—was deliberately composed to bolster his portrayal of himself as insane. No one properly connected to reality would do or say what he claimed. He was clearly constructing a portrait of someone psychotic—irrational, unduly trusting and dependent on the police officers interviewing him.

"It's all nonsense. It's all part of his play to advance an NCR defence," Coleen told the Turners early in the prosecution. "You'll hear that term a lot. It stands for 'Not Criminally Responsible due to a mental disorder.' In American movies, they might call it 'not guilty by reason of insanity'—that sort of thing."

"It can't work though," Sheila argued. "He can't just get up in court and lie and promise to stay on his pills and then walk away like nothing happened."

Coleen nodded as if she was swallowing something whole. "He'd still be held in custody even with an NCR verdict. He'd be held indefinitely in a psychiatric hospital instead of in a penitentiary. They wouldn't let him out until they thought it was safe for him to rejoin the public. That could take from one year to the rest of his life. Who knows? If it comes to that, his time in custody will be out of our hands. But let's not get ahead of ourselves. We have evidence he wasn't acutely mentally ill when the murder was committed. He was ill before and he's been ill since then but he was working and healthy and his ability to understand the consequences of his actions was just fine the last time he saw Tricia. Look at the elaborate plans he made to move her body, and the way he understood he had to go home and get what he needed to live and work somewhere else before he left town. The story about demons and stabbing at her ear—we don't buy that. It's a detail he added himself to inject acute mental illness into the story after the fact. All of that—that's cunning. It's not how someone suffering a psychotic break would behave. We'll have expert witnesses come and testify to that. See, we have evidence and we have a prosecutor who has successfully dismantled NCR defences in the past. And for once, the legal onus is on Finnemore's defence. It's up to defence to prove he was mentally diseased, not up to us to prove he wasn't. See, we have many, many reasons to hope for him to be held fully responsible for second degree murder."

Finnemore's version of the story, the prosecution's objections to it—it's all on the public record now. The story was told in open court during the Preliminary Hearing, not with the drama of true crime television but in the monotone of legal proceedings, words carefully chosen to be nothing but informative—no inflection, nothing inflammatory that could get the whole thing thrown out as too prejudicial toward the accused person. Nowhere is Canadian politeness more pronounced than when the state is trying someone on charges of horrendous misbehaviour. During the hearing, Joshua Lund laid out the Crown's evidence of second degree murder and offering an indignity to a dead body while the second defence lawyer to be on the case—the one Finnemore fired before hiring Dean Orenchuk—did a perfectly competent job of complaining about all of it.

The Preliminary Hearing seemed like waste of time to the Turners but, Coleen explained, the point was to see if the case was strong enough to deserve a trial. Coleen with her plain speech, her steadiness, her black leather pumps Morgan recognized from the modest department store in the mall—she makes more sense to Morgan than anyone else in the justice system. But none of Coleen's charms work on Sheila.

Marc Turner, Father of Victim, takes his own different approach to the prosecution of Brett Finnemore. He believes Finnemore's defence, accepts that he must be mentally ill past the point of understanding there were never any demons in Tricia's ear. Marc doesn't live with the rest of the family anymore but with a woman named Julie, out at Lake Wabamun in a cabin that's more of a shanty with a toilet that's more of a compost bin. He doesn't see his grown children often, doesn't drive into the city for court dates or for anything else that violates his principles.

"Someone let Brett Finnemore down," he has told the news microphones. "All of society has let him down. He paid that deficit forward to our Tricia, and to the rest of us. But it's got to stop with me. It's not moving a single inch forward from here. I've got to see that young man lifted up."

These are the kinds of soundbites Marc has produced for the crime reporters. By profession, he is a social worker, supplementing his government job with a part-time inspirational speaking circuit and a self-published book called *Healing the Light Within*. He is another one of the people made famous by Tricia's death. When he is on television, the caption below his face reads "Marc Turner Forgives Daughter's Alleged Killer."

His celebrity started in the same place as Sheila's, at a folding table at the first police press conference after Tricia's death. Underneath the table, out of the range of the cameras, he held his long-divorced wife's hand as the police officer read the prepared statement. No one but Morgan noticed.

"Don't take stuff like that seriously, Morgo," Tod told her. "Being nice when things are going wrong is something he does for money. He's a crisis gigolo."

Their daughter's death made Sheila into someone who talks about advocacy and answers. Marc bolted in the opposite direction, becoming someone who talks about solace and serenity. It's as if they are bound by a formal agreement—each of them planted at the opposite poles of suffering. The aftermath of Tricia's death was neatly, perfectly divided between them, as if it had been planned and codified in their divorce papers, stamped and filed at the courthouse. It was transparent—embarrassing—the two of them acting as the anima and animus of parental pain, something out of the Joseph Campbell books they had bought together when they were university students in love and bell-bottoms.

It is not only hackneyed but badly executed. Marc Turner—he is a poor-man's Reverend Len Vreend. Everyone knows Reverend Vreend. Like the Turners, he is also the father of a murdered child, a teenaged son who was killed in a copy-cat school shooting on the tenth anniversary of the Columbine High School massacre. A younger kid who hardly knew Vreend Junior shot him to death in the atrium of a small-town hockey arena. There would have been more casualties if a former high school football star, now a municipal maintenance worker, hadn't rushed and sacked the shooter and got control of the rifle with his bare hands. He shrugged when the reporters asked him their hero questions.

"It was just a .22."

The Vreend family was churchy, of course, but in the media storm that came after the shooting, there was no confused, well-meant, half-true Christian martyr story attached to Vreend Junior—not like there was with those girls in the library at Columbine. The Vreend story is simple, clear—an old story about someone killed for stepping into the wrong place at the wrong time, someone hurrying to hockey practice a little too late. It is a story with no sex in it, no grownups, no women—not much like Tricia Turner's story at all.

Reverend Vreend worked to let his son remain an ordinary kid, a dead but ordinary kid, which is saintly enough. The protagonist of the Chinook Arena shooting story became Vreend himself. His business was sermons and prayers and when his son died, he went to work. Reverend Vreend preached everywhere—at schools and churches, for conferences and committees, in person, on television. His message was forgiveness and love, told in prayers and readings from the Bible—almost familiar to almost everyone. The news people followed, waiting for him to get teenagers to cry on camera. It wasn't Vreend's fault. Reporters followed the Turners when their child died too. The news people, they were just going to work, the same as Vreend.

The first time Morgan saw Reverend Vreend on television was two days after his son was killed. He was speaking at a memorial service in the arena where the shooting had happened. Vreend Junior's classmates—high-school kids, and their parents—all bereaved and afraid, were seated behind the white hockey boards. Vreend Senior stood on the cement floor where the ice should have been, talking into the lapel microphone the television crew had clipped to him. The local network affiliate was broadcasting the service live all over the province. In the arena, a big screen behind Vreend showed a larger, fuzzier image of him moving and talking. He wasn't angry—said nothing about life sentences or slaughters. His said he forgave the boy who killed his son—said it differently than Marc Turner, but said it nonetheless. Dante's old *Inferno* church might be all hell and damnation, but Vreend's church was about trying not to feel miserable even when feeling miserable is the only thing that makes sense. That was Vreend's message at his son's memorial—ironic, impossible peace.

He stood on the buffed concrete and preached. He said, "Let us pray" the way some pastors still do. But he didn't pray, didn't even bow his head. He looked into the crowd, one corner of his smile twitching like a glitch in Morgan's television signal as she watched from her living room in another city. Something in the memorial service had changed—the tone, the light—everything transfigured. Reverend Vreend beckoned toward the bleachers for the crowd to follow him out of the rink. The cameras lost sight of him for a moment when he pushed the double doors open and stopped in the arena's atrium, in front of the trophy case, the spot where his son had bled onto the floor. On camera, Bible in hand, he raised his arms, opened his mouth, and performed an exorcism.

That's what it was called in the newspapers. That's what the television people called it when they reported it again on the late edition. "Father of slain Alberta teen, the Reverend Len Vreend, was at the Chinook Arena today to conduct an exorcism on the spot where his son was fatally shot by a schoolmate late last week…"

Only the television cameras—glassy, mechanical eyes—kept looking directly at Vreend while he exorcised the arena. Everyone else visible in the crowd on Morgan's TV screen—the cry-weary girls and the boys with the hoods of their sweatshirts draped over their eyes—hid their faces.

"Evil has entered into this place," Reverend Vreend said, "and it must be sent out."

He bossed the evil, cast it out, lifted his Bible above his head—calling on holy beings, rebuking unholy ones. The Bible in his hand rose and fell, sweeping through the air of the atrium as if evil was a bumblebee, caught indoors, to be shooed away. The news clips didn't show all of the rite, of course. When Morgan saw the exorcism the second, third, and fourth times it was heavily edited, cutting in and out. Since then, she has looked everywhere for a record of all Vreend had said, some sign of whether the exorcism worked. No one seems to know.

Tod would not talk about it. "I never seen no exorcism. And neither have you." Bad grammar is his exclamation mark.

Morgan has not met Reverend Vreend. She has imagined it—standing with him at the arena's trophy case, asking him all of her questions—but with Tricia between them, with Vreend Junior between them, a meeting might be a mess, every grief-pornographer journalist's greatest wish.

It is possible that Marc Turner has sought him out and met him, but Morgan doubts it. Marc says God is a metaphor from the monomyth and he is happy enough to leave it that way. The last two times Morgan has seen her father on television, he was wearing a headset microphone and pacing onstage. Forgiveness is Marc's bonus pay cheque, his sweet side-hustle. He has never exorcised anything, but he leads soul-healing weekend retreats, deep in the woods on Julie's family's land along the lake. Marc has established himself as a mentor and coach for people more than usually aware of the wrongs they've been done. He gets them to talk, sing, cry, hug each other, bathe in the lake, and thank and thank and thank him. Sometimes, he takes the show on the road—calls it a workshop because words like "revival" tend to rankle people nowadays.

That's what Sheila said when she watched Marc's latest TV interview, the one he did the day Finnemore was first arraigned in court. She laughed, leaned into the screen, squinting. "What is he wearing?"

It wasn't what Marc was wearing that was strange but how he was wearing it. He was dressed in a plain white shirt—the same kind of shirt the prosecutor wears when he is at work in a normal suit instead of his robes. Marc wore the shirt with the top buttons undone, no necktie. He spread the collar wide open, smoothing it all the way to its points with the palms of his hands so it rested along the base of his neck in two flattened cotton wings, white like a dove flying at his throat.

News directors don't send crews to film clips of Marc's workshops anymore, not like in the beginning. He can hardly make anyone cry unless they desperately want to all on their own. Marc's forgiveness of Tricia's killer— it is becoming old news. Sheila's anger is always raw and steaming, irresolvable. Her story is tenacity—chasing Finnemore toward a crushing, punishing destiny she has already publicly denounced as insufficient. When she and Marc divided up their archetypes, he chose the wrong side. His story is of cooling and moving on—a loud, public claim of letting go. Soon, he will have to stop talking about it, stop posing for it, stop pleading for it, and do it.

4

It was a mistake for Gillian to say anything to Paul about nineteenth century Japanese armaments on their way to the courthouse. While she was parking the car, he was finishing his breakfast—the chocolate bar he had found in the bottom of Gillian's bag—and folding its foil wrapper into the shape of a star. It looked enough like a cartoon ninja weapon for her to say, "I don't think I understand throwing stars, Paulie. Were they even real outside of marital arts movies? Seems to me like they wouldn't do much damage."

Paul tossed the foil star across the front seat of the car at her. "What, *shurikens*? They're real but mostly used as distraction tactics, so you can confuse the enemy long enough to get in there with swords and whatnot. And they're actually pretty good for that..."

He is still talking about weapons in fine *Dungeons and Dragons Player's Handbook* detail—not throwing stars anymore but halberds—as they step inside from the street to stand in line at the courthouse security screening area. Loud and fast, he's saying, "Sure, a halberd's unwieldy but you need all that shaft-length. How else are you going to grapple with an attacker who's way up on horseback?"

Gillian eyes the courthouse sheriffs, prays Paul stops using word like "assassin" and "plunge line." It doesn't seem to matter. None of the uniformed guards behind the stainless-steel tables flinches as Paul talks on and on, tugging off his belt and dropping it into a plastic bin with his jacket and keys, startling himself as his metal personal effects clatter against each other.

Gillian clears security without any wands or rubber-gloved gropings. The guards take more time with Paul. It isn't because of the weapons chit-chat. Gillian can forget but the truth is Paul is scary. If they were strangers, and she was walking alone and saw him coming toward her, she would notice, watch, worry. But they are not strangers. And it is when Gillian walks alone in the city that people stop her. They ask for money, directions, sex. Their voices get loud, they open their arms. Paul's presence neutralizes all of that. Gillian never feels safer walking through the city than when she is walking with scary, hairy, jittery Paul. Together they have joked about people assuming she must be his "worker"—someone obligated by a job or a philanthropic agency to walk him through his worst days. She's not. Gillian travels with Paul for love. This man is her family, her other brother.

At the end of the security conveyor belt, Paul is getting his kit back together, nervously but graciously bearing with the indignity of dressing in an open public space, jabbing the end of his belt through the loops of his pants, pulling his jacket over his shoulders. "Gigi, hey, how's my man-bun looking?"

She spins him between her hands, pausing at his back to pick at the lint clinging to the loose fabric between his shoulder blades. "Breathtaking."

They walk to a wall of television screens like the ones hung in airports to show flights arriving and departing. The screens are actually displaying today's court appearances. They are difficult to read—the names listed in something misleadingly close to alphabetical order, but not quite. There's his name: Paul Lund, Courtroom 356. Paul Lund, troubled younger brother of Joshua Lund, the prosecutor who, at this moment, is on the third floor running an aggravated assault trial.

Gillian knows this already. When she realized it, in Josh and Leanne's kitchen after dinner on Sunday night, she had laughed. "As if, you guys. Ya can't make this stuff up."

Joshua's trial is going into its third day even though the accused already confessed to the non-fatal stabbing, right there on the witness stand during Josh's cross-examination yesterday afternoon. The admission was made with the clichéd phrasing of an onscreen confession the accused does not realize he is copying from an old noir film.

"What do you want me to say? You want me to say I stabbed him? Fine, I stabbed him. There, you happy?"

Three storeys below the trial, Gillian stands at Paul's side, glancing at his face, reading the mood of his new state of twitching quiet, as if beneath his clothing he is covered in hives he must not scratch. There are no more weapons dissertations. A woman passes through their line of sight as they stand in front of the screens. She is walking backwards, calling to someone lagging behind her. "No, no more. Just shut up and serve your fourteen days. Suck it up."

The man beside Gillian has the same name, same flesh and bones as the boy she met so long ago she doesn't remember meeting him at all. Paul and Josh were once just as cute as one another, clicking at video games, listening to The Smiths in their parents' basement before the band became a rom-com soundtrack, blasting them loud, as if they were Metallica. As their father would say, the brothers have both put some rough mileage on themselves since then—rough miles of different kinds, with different effects. Still, if Paul and Josh were to stand face to face, chins level, eyes straight ahead, everything would match—eyebrows, jawlines, noses, lips—it would all line up. Their brotherhood is as obvious as it is now unlikely. In this place, it is also unspeakable. If Josh and Paul happen to see each other here, today, they will nod and pass without a word.

Paul and Gillian queue at the case management office counter with the rest of the self-represented accused people who can't afford lawyers but are not yet in enough jeopardy of going to jail to qualify for Legal Aid. The social worker coming down the line with a pen and a list, triaging, is someone they have spoken to before. Gillian nudges Paul, "Hey, it's that guy."

Paul's muscles contract all at once, from head to foot, as if he is about to bolt. But what he says is, "Oh, yeah."

"He probably already knows if you've been cleared for the Mental Health Diversion programme."

Paul hums, taps one foot against the floor in cut time.

They are at the courthouse today to answer for trouble Paul got into last fall, when he became convinced his anti-psychotic medications were actually what was making him psychotic and quietly stopped taking them. Everyone hopes Paul's "rock bottom" was the concrete floor of a cell in the downtown police station, his wrists zipped together, his untreated paranoid schizophrenia burning at full throttle.

The day of his arrest, Paul's mind was lit with hallucinations and fear, his body hungry enough to go outside, to stand on the sidewalk of a soup kitchen, trying, trying to wait quietly for food. Someone spoke to him and he was arguing, fighting with a tiny, withered down-and-outer half his age. The man, mouthy but scared, panicked and hit Paul in the jaw with a weak, but hard and scabby fist. Paul chased him across the parking lot, swearing he'd kill him, before sitting to sob on the curb. That was it. Even as an un-medicated paranoid schizophrenic reeling from a blow to the face, that was the extent of Paul Lund's criminal rampage.

No one else waiting for lunch outside the soup kitchen would admit to seeing Paul get hit. Seeing meant knowing, and knowing would have meant telling, and telling would have meant being here in court today, getting felt up in security, stripping off clothing, standing up as a witness, being asked to produce a home address. In fairness, Paul wouldn't have done it for any of them. But the staff inside the kitchen had heard Paul holler the death threat.

They invoked their zero tolerance of abuse policy, took the chance to prove to the entire lunch crowd how serious it was, and Paul was charged with the little-known crime of uttering death threats.

When the police found him, they asked, "You wouldn't really hurt that old guy, would you?"

If Paul had been a typical hothead street fighter, he would have assured the police he would never hurt anyone. He would have apologized, offered promises, and the matter might have ended. But Paul is sick—doctor's note crazy, as the family calls it among themselves. Alone, no lawyer, tripping on paranoia, he paced his living room floor between the stacks of flattened cardboard boxes he cannot throw away, picking at the cuticles of his fingernails until they bled, telling the police, "Yeah, I would hurt him. If he came around my place, if I had to, I would kill him. I have ways."

What Paul meant to say glares at his sister through what he did say. He was speaking of fear. He was afraid the swat on the jaw outside the soup kitchen was the leading edge of some vast, monumental threat, something dangerous and important enough to change his life forever. He was telling the police how scared he was, pleading for help, asking them to save him so he would not need to go to extreme lengths to save himself.

The police heard none of it. Instead of crisis counselling, Paul got handcuffed. Instead of a refill on his lapsed Zyprexa prescription, he got a recognizance and a court date.

Gillian read the officers' notes in Paul's police file—the disclosure package the court had given him to take to a lawyer. With a prosecutor for a brother, Paul should have the very best legal advice. Only, that's not it at all. Joshua Lund works for the Crown, his brother's opponent, making him the last person Paul could talk to about his criminal charges. Josh is in the service of Her Majesty, the Queen of England, and he can't help criminals evade her justice or she could throw a fit, throw him out, and he could spend the rest of his career rubber stamping residential mortgages. Instead of all that, Gillian walked the line just short of practising law without a licence, writing articulate letters in her ornate graduate school English for Paul to sign, informed by the insights into criminal law she has absorbed from Josh, asking him hypothetical questions they both knew were nothing of the sort. She wrote the letters, came rapping at the window of Paul's basement apartment to wake him up, drove him to the courthouse, and, when she had to, held both of his hands in hers, fighting his nervous tic of over-grooming his nails, keeping his fingers from ripping each other apart.

"Take my hands, Sweetie. Take mine. Hold on. We're still okay."

For now, Paul is not afraid of his medicine. It has been almost a year since he last called the ambulance ranting about his feet rotting off. The tiny burning comets and dragons he used to see tearing through his peripheral vision have nearly vanished—and when they do appear, usually when he is in bed, motionless, his head is on his pillow, right before he falls to sleep or shortly after he wakes up, he knows to reassure himself that everyone is safe, no one is talking about him, he has not been made a character in a book he will never read. What he sees are hallucinations, what he almost hears are the effects of a disease, symptoms not much different in kind than a runny nose or a rash of pustules.

When the police told Paul he had to appear in court, and he finally called his family for help, Gillian discovered he was also on the verge of homelessness, bankruptcy, everything. After filling out forms, tracking down scraps of mislaid paperwork, and escorting him to appointments for months on end, Gillian succeeded in getting him a disability pension. He has money for groceries and doesn't need to take his chances at the soup kitchens anymore. The rent on his basement suite is subsidized and the landlord has stopped serving him with the monthly eviction notices Paul always ignored. His affairs are peaceful and stable, quiet enough for Paul to fall into the arms of his medications and sleep for fourteen hours every day.

This has been the account of Paul's tumble into the pit as Gillian would have told it. The account Paul would tell is different. Gillian would have no place in it. The world around him is only around him. That world spans no more than the reach of both his arms, the universe no further than the scope of his eyesight. His break with reality cracks along the fault-line of his belief that everything— everything—shifts and drifts in sympathy with his tiniest thought or action. He brings the lightning, plagues and famine, fire falling from the sky or rising molten from the earth. He is all four horsemen, all seven seals. And once the cataclysms begin, he fuels them but cannot control them. It is a manic fiction and an awful burden.

In his mind, Gillian is even farther out of Paul's universe than Josh. She knows it from the way he stops thinking about her as soon as she is out of sight, the way he never calls to tell her when he gets word one of their applications has been approved or denied, and the way the last thing he would ever think to give her is thanks. It's okay with her that he has never said thanks. But it would be more okay if he did.

The last of what remains to be dealt with in Rock-Bottom-Paulie's blast zone is settling his criminal charges—that and getting his hair cut.

The courthouse social worker with the docket list stops beside them in the line of self-represented accused people. He squints at Paul. "Hey, here's a familiar face." He finds Paul's name on the list. The application they brought to have Paul's criminal charge dealt with in the Mental Health Diversion programme instead of through a criminal trial has been approved. After Paul completes some special probation and counselling, the Crown will withdraw the matter as if nothing ever happened.

Gillian hops, gives a restrained courthouse cheer. "Paulie, you're not getting a criminal record." She folds both of her arms around one of Paul's.

"He still has to complete his counselling."

"Of course he will. That's easy. Right?"

Paul and Gillian climb the steps to the upper floors. In a docket courtroom away from their brother, they wait to be called by the court clerk. This may be the last time they will ever be in this building together as anything other than Josh's fans. Maybe, Gillian thinks, she will bring Paul to watch the Finnemore trial when it begins. The Not Criminally Responsible defence Finnemore is advancing is a little like what they have done with Paul today, though it's best not to bring it to his attention.

"So how is Mental Health Diversion different from pleading Not Criminally Responsible by reason of a mental disorder?" Gillian asked Josh, months ago, when he risked offending the Queen by suggesting Gillian look into applying to have Paul diverted.

Josh was reading a case, lying flat on his back on his living room couch—black leather for easy clean-up. A big crawling baby clambered along on his shins. Josh rubbed his eyes, adjusted his legs to keep the baby from toppling onto the rug. "It's not all that different in nature. The difference is mostly in the seriousness of the crimes to be considered. I mean, someone like Brett Finnemore, the shopping-cart murder guy, he's in too much trouble to apply for Mental Health Diversion. But he can ask the court to find him Not Criminally Responsible and wind up in a high se-curity mental health facility instead of a penitentiary."

This was strange to her. Incarceration is incarceration. Josh had shrugged. "Well, if Finnemore still considers himself a ladies' man, a hospital is definitely a better place for him to meet women. That and he could give up the crazy act and get a review board to let him out in as little as a year. Remember that guy who beheaded and started eating his seatmate on the Greyhound to Winnipeg a while back? He was found NCR and now, properly medicated, he's a free man."

In the courtroom, mental health diverted Paul is ordered to sign papers and attend counselling. The judge calls him forward to stand and agree to everything, out loud, on the record. And that's it. He will report to the court in three months, one more appearance, and the file will be closed for good.

Gillian and Paul's post-court ritual is ice cream. Usually it's a consolation after a miserable morning of disappointment and delay. Today, it is a celebration. Paul eats his black raspberry ripple and tells Gillian the entire plotline of an indie horror movie he knows she will never watch—a gory one about a demon apocalypse. There is a twist at the end, revealing the entire show as a horror movie rendering of Pascal's Wager. Gillian laughs so hard she bends over the table, getting someone else's caramel syrup residue in her hair.

Paul grins. "Yeah, I thought you'd like that."

It's a good day. Gillian texts Josh to tell him what's happened. He is back at his trial, the ringer on his phone turned off.

Paul's ice cream is gone. He is smoothing the nap of his corduroy jacket back and forth under his palm, confabulating all the clever ways the prosecutors must have played and manipulated him before they were satisfied and let him into the Mental Health Diversion programme. Gillian doesn't disagree though the fact is Paul's matter was a low complexity, level one criminal charge. No one in Josh's crisis-driven office would have given it more than a few minutes' thought.

He tugs the elastic out of his hair and shakes his head. His hair falls, limp and stringy, past his shoulders. "Who am I kidding?" he says. "My man-bun makes me look like Mom."

They will spend the rest of the afternoon at his apartment. Gillian will offer to cut his hair, and he will decline. She will offer to tidy up, and he will accept, looking away as she does him the service of sneakily tossing out all but one of the plastic Slurpee cups he cannot risk pitching into the bin himself. She will wash a sink of dishes, and Paul will stack them in his cupboards, but not before cuing up some tunes from his old CD collection. He will stand with his sister in the tiny, crumby kitchen, his singing voice sounding high above her head, the same tenor as that of the high school boy in their parents' basement, so sweet—in spite of the crush of the smallest, scariest of universes—still so sweet.

5

A massive wild fire is burning in the north, consuming not only woods and camps but the city of Fort McMurray itself—100,000 people evacuating through ash and flames. Their traffic has arrived in Edmonton—full-sized diesel pickup trucks jammed with pillows, bottled water, children with no coats, miserable pets. Smoke came after them, drifting into Edmonton in a single afternoon—filtering the light of a ragged yellow sun, deepening it to red, shrinking it into a disc, its edges tightened into perfect roundness. In Edmonton, one million people are caught in the long grey plume of smoke satellites have been photographing from outer space. From orbit, it looks like a slow, floating comet caught inside the Earth's atmosphere. From the Earth, the comet is felt more than seen—a dry, stinging fog with a smell not like campfires but house fires. It is the burning of human-made objects—foam mattresses, pressboard furniture, clothing and groceries, gasified and gone. It is something like the smell of fires lit and controlled in city dumps—melted glue and poly-vinyl-garbage.

The smoke and stench have seeped inside the bus

during Morgan Turner's commute home from work. It is the smell of her childhood with Tricia and Tod and both of her parents, of the time they lived high in forest fire country, in Fort McMurray themselves. Is their old house still standing—the one with the harvest gold siding and the bay window, set on a corner at the entry to a cul-de-sac in Thickwood Heights? She asked Tod if he thinks it's still there, and he said not even the people who own that house now would know for sure if it's burned down—not yet.

During their Fort McMurray days, Marc Turner worked for Eye Knack. That's all Morgan knew. She could tell it was a strange job—one of the few someone without steel-toed boots could work. Compared to the other fathers on their crescent, Marc's Eye Knack shift was funny—the same five days on, the same two days off, over and over again. No one talked about where the "eye" in Eye Knack was, or what it might have had a "knack" for.

Sheila's job, on the other hand, was easy to understand. She was a nurse—teacher, hair dresser, secretary, nurse—one of the real jobs.

When the bogs and muskeg north and east of town froze solid, and Eye Knack sent Marc to ride the winter roads, a four-wheel drive truck would appear parked outside their yellow house. It was Eye Knack's vehicle, dingy baby-blue, with a decal on its front door, a modest maple leaf and rows of white lettering: "Indian and Northern Affairs Canada."

Morgan had been able to read for years by the time she finally squinted through the dry, dirty frost on the living room window at the writing on the Eye Knack truck and read it out loud to just herself, in something like Tricia's voice. It said, Indian and Northern Affairs Canada—I-N-A-C, INAC, not Eye Knack.

Whatever it was, without any oil company money, INAC kept the Turners the poorest family on the crescent. Anyone could tell with one look at their driveway: no boat, no camper, no dirt bikes, not even a snowmobile. As long as the INAC truck was parked downtown in the government lot, it was just cars for the Turner family. Sometimes people get sentimental, silly, trying to say kids don't notice stuff like—stuff. They're wrong. Kids notice things, little things, everything. Morgan's days were long enough, her world was small enough, for all of it to be measured and weighed.

For one thing, she could tell their television didn't work like other people's. The Turners had no cable, no satellite. All they saw on the single screen in their house was the static of the CBC—Peter Mansbridge and Ernie Coombs and hundreds of tiny hockey players beaming through their bodies on broadcast signals.

First-world deprivation is boredom—fat, grey afternoons. Morgan, Tricia, and Tod—they weren't sick or hungry, but they were bored. Don't try to say everyone's bored and we're all responsible for making our own fun. It was minus forty degrees outside.

Marc Turner tried to make it up to his kids in the media room at the district INAC office. On Saturday mornings, when the neighbourhood children were watching robot cartoons or breaking their necks on their dads' snowmobiles, Marc's kids were in the INAC office watching whatever they could find in the flat tin cans of 16mm film in the media room.

The INAC office still reeked of tobacco from the 1980s. The walls of the media room were yellowed and made of a wallboard so soft Morgan could scratch it open with her fingernail if no one was watching. And on a table—one corner propped on a stack of policy manuals to make it level—was a film projector aimed at a bare wall. The films were mostly footage of people with cold ears trudging through snow, maybe with a dog or two. They looked like they were doing the same boring things Morgan always did. They weren't, of course. The mumbly soundtracks shaky with ripples, the consonants rolled off the edges of the words, explained what was better— important—about their walks, though Morgan doesn't remember what it was.

There was only one film in the media room worth watching. The Turner kids called it "The Fire Movie." Its real title, Morgan would find out much later, is *He Comes Without Calling*. It's about a nice, normal family and a black-robed, hooded, blue-white-faced spectre—the personification of death by fire. The spectre does not apologize, but he does explain that he has no choice but to stalk the family, like a hunter in winter, while they sleep in their tidy Reserve bungalow. At night, he inspects their house, narrating in a formal tenor, finding fire hazards everywhere. Their house was a lot like the Turner's—small, with a floor that looked cold except for where a brown braided rug was laid in the living room. Marc and Sheila had the same rug, in the same space in their living room. Morgan hadn't stepped on it in months.

No matter how Tod remembers it, Morgan has not lived her life completely outside of horror movies. Maybe no one left alive remembers her horror movie, but that is something different from her never having had one. Horror—as far as Morgan knows, it is the human condition, no exceptions. It is true for Tod and Tricia and for their little sister too. This fire prevention movie was Morgan's horror movie. It was a long time ago, it was only art, it was nothing much—not compared to Tricia getting killed, or Tod winding up at a slaughterhouse. None of that means it wasn't real.

"You are not going to let them watch it again," Sheila told Marc when he stood up to take the kids for another Saturday morning at the INAC office.

He knew what she meant. But he said, "Let them watch what?"

"That Ingmar-Bergman-comes-to-the-Reserve-show."

"They ask for it every time. They beg me for it."

"No. It is making her crazy." Sheila jerked her chin toward where the kids were tangling in the boot closet behind him. She was not talking about Tricia. "And that makes the rest of us crazy. She's up all night. You can hear her creeping around, checking on the furnace, un-plugging all the lamps. It has to stop."

Morgan was going crazy. It was true even before her

mother said it aloud. Morgan was a paranoid wreck, every night, and The Fire Movie was to blame. She was padding around in the dark, sniffing the air for a whiff of gas, sneaking into bed with ever-angry teenaged Tricia, crying if Sheila shut their bedroom door, terrified their lives would flame into a scene from the movie—the one where the spectre first comes into the house, appearing in front of a closed door, materializing out of a jet of white smoke.

Outside the boot closet, Marc committed to the argument. "Come on, Sheila. It's just a public service message, a fire safety movie—a really effective fire safety movie."

Whatever it was, it scared Morgan more than anything she knew, from the first blast of the trombones in the opening credits all the way to the ending shot of a heap of white spruce boughs piled on a little girl's grave. The fire, the spectre—they proved what all kids suspect. Normal houses are monsters' houses. There is no other kind of house. We don't see or hear them come, but they are with us anyway, in the dark, moving through the spaces where we eat and sleep and sit around bored.

The argument and the delay were excuse enough for Tricia to denounce the entire family, kick off her boots, and slam back to her bedroom. It happened all the time.

The rest of them—Marc, Tod, Morgan—they drove down the hill and into the lower town-site, arrived at the INAC office, rode the elevator to the second floor.

The door opened to the smell of old smoke. It was no emergency, no forest fire, no house fire, but grownup smoke—white and slow—the kind adults kindled on the edges of their lips. Smokers had to go outside now, but the buildings kept traces of smoke in their carpets, furniture, curtains.

In the INAC office, the lights were off in the media room. The projector was rattling The Fire Movie against the wall. Marc was out of sight, in the next room, writing letters to FAX. Tod twisted the lens out and then back into focus, their opening ritual.

Trombones—and then the lights came on. Light travels the same speed all the time and there's nothing anyone can do about it. Everyone knows that. This light felt faster anyway, the difference between a step and a kick. In the light was Sheila, standing in the doorway, her coat undone, crooked, its belt hanging untied at her sides.

"Off—now," she said.

She'd come to save her daughter. It was love. It was awful.

The film's horns kept blaring despite the light. Sheila lunged past the threshold, into the room, tugged the projector's power cord out of the wall.

"Now."

Something in Morgan cooled and hardened like lava in the ocean crusting into solid rock, or the calcifying shell of a newborn creature moving through seawater.

Marc was calling down the hallway. "You guys, what's with the burning plastic smell?"

Tod fumbled with the lank length of the projector's power cord. "Mom shut the movie off without letting the fan cool the bulb down."

Pushing past all of them, Marc pulled the reel of film from the projector's arm. It came out of the aperture gate sideways, shriveled, melted.

Marc and Sheila mended it with scissors and cellophane tape and shouting. A few seconds of the snow plough scene were lost. Otherwise, Marc said The Fire Movie was fine. No need to report the damage. "A bit shaky, a bit bouncy, kind of a rough ride, but not ruined."

And then, when the snow still hadn't quite melted off the Turners' front lawn, before forest fire season started again, the family moved south—just drove away, like everyone does. Morgan's horror movie was scorched, patched, slid into a can, and left behind as if no one would ever know what they had done.

Marc kept saying he couldn't stay with INAC, where his work did not make a difference. A difference was something to be made—like noise or toast. Morgan's parents talked about leaving as part of their nightly routine, in the kitchen, over boiling pots of pasta—their lackluster cooking—as she lay under the table, matching her fingerprints to the greasy spots on the underside of the wood where she wiped her hands during dinner. It went on for months before Sheila agreed to let him quit.

Outside grownup Morgan's bus, the city they moved to from Fort McMurray will shut its windows and wait all night for rain to rinse the ash out of the sky, back into the carbon cycle. This year's forest fire's terrestrial smoke-comet must reach all the way to Wabamun Lake, where her father lives now. He will breathe it into his body too.

Marc Turner will smell and taste the smoke and think of INAC, evacuating Reserves over rough back roads, the old disaster stories of the elders, films disintegrating unwatched in cans. For a moment, he may remember everything.

Tod's car is in the shop getting a new radiator, Sheila is home in the dark with a migraine headache, and only Morgan is left to ferry her car back home after Tod drives himself to work in it during the rush of the abattoir's shift change.

"See ya, Morgo," he says, heaving himself out of the Hyundai. At his size, the car fits him more like a suit of armour than a vehicle. He bails out of the driver's side door and nearly rolls onto the wet pavement of the parking lot like a stuntman making an escape. He is on his feet, moving toward a steel door in the slaughterhouse wall.

Morgan scoots over the parking break, pulls the driver's seat ahead far enough for her to lean against the steering wheel, bending to see the billboard mounted on the roof of the factory. She flicks the windshield wipers, clearing away the rain still falling, still flushing forest fire smoke out of the sky. Through the glass, she reads the sign telling her Freibergs is always hiring new staff. Beside the black letters spelling out this message is a picture of a man in a hairnet—airbrush-perfect skin and eyebrows—smiling like he is the luckiest man alive. Standing behind him, grinning over his shoulder, cut and pasted from somewhere else, is a young woman wearing glasses so finely rimmed Morgan can hardly see them.

The woman doesn't have a hairnet. Her hair is tied in a sleek pony tail—a clerical hairdo. Secretaries and receptionists—to girls working in cheap restaurants those careers are charmed. No aprons, no nametags, hours and hours passing without having to wash their hands. No one means for a "pink ghetto" to be something nice but it looks like cotton candy from Morgan's fast food dish-pit.

Inquire within, she mouths as if she is reading, as if the words on the Freibergs billboard don't actually say, "Come Join Us." The human resources people composed the billboard copy to sound friendly and fun, but it reads like a membership pitch for a cult. And it's working.

Morgan rolls down her window. Light rain speckles her skin, but she is thinking of smoke, frayed wires tucked under heavy rugs, cairns of cut spruce boughs. She wants a new horror movie. No more haughty, cloaked ghosts sneaking around the kitchen while everyone is asleep and helpless. No more nobody's fire marshals. She wants a proper horror movie—one with a storyline she can watch unfolding with a beginning, a middle, and someday maybe, an end. Tricia's horror movie is a courtroom drama now—too slow, too caught up in paper and protocols. The ending has been spoiled, anyway. What is left for Morgan to sample is Tod's slasher movie—hoofs and guts, everyone a cog in a terrifying machine, always awake and afoot.

She is walking on the pavement toward the main entrance of the factory, not Tod's steel employee side-door—not yet. Morgan goes to the glass doors meant for salespeople and migrant workers with newly upgraded work visas. Rainwater wicks into the canvas of her shoes. Her heart feels smaller and quicker than usual, set slightly higher in her chest. The new horror movie is opening, its theme played on oboes, and strings tuned almost to breaking.

6

It was winter when a man broke into an RV storage compound, lit a dozen holiday trailers on fire, jammed a screwdriver into the ignition of an all-terrain quad, and drove it as far away as he could before the adrenaline metabolized out of his bloodstream and he realized the mesh of his gloves had melted and fused with the flesh of his hands and arms. He has been in custody at the Edmonton Remand Centre ever since he was discharged from the hospital, waiting for today, for his trial at the Court of Queen's Bench. The Crown's case will be simple—security camera footage, and no civilian witnesses other than the man who owned the stolen quad standing up to say, Yes, this was his vehicle and, No, he did not give the burning man permission to drive it off into the night.

The defence case will not be simple. They are calling a defence of Not Criminally Responsible for reason of a mental disorder—NCR, the same defence as Brett Finnemore's.

The RV arsonist story was all over the news this morning—as anything the news people can call an inferno usually is—and it has drawn Morgan out of her mother's living room and onto a bus bound for the courthouse. She hasn't told Sheila, or Tod, or anyone where she is spending her morning. Maybe, she thinks, they haven't told her either, and they will all meet at the courtroom, by surprise, and laugh so hard they might get asked to take their noise out into the hallway. What is more likely is that Morgan will sit by herself, quietly figuring out what an NCR defence looks like—seeing if a lunatic who inconvenienced a bunch of posh camping enthusiasts but didn't actually hurt anyone but himself can make one work. It's something like a dress rehearsal for Finnemore's trial, especially since the prosecutors' office has sent in its resident expert on NCR defences, Joshua Lund.

Whatever Morgan learns about the justice system today will be far more enlightening than spending another day at home obsessively fixated on Freibergs, as if the factory is someone she is in love with who doesn't love her back and can't be bothered to call and tell her so. It has been one week since she left a job application with the frizzy-haired white lady working as the Freibergs receptionist. Nothing Morgan wrote on the application was very impressive—restaurant jobs, one summer at a convenience store, a high school diploma, and one semester at a college. Not even her handwriting was good.

There are several sets of stairs from the street level of the courthouse to the upper floors where the courtrooms are. One is meant to be showy—glass and bronze-coloured metal in the centre of an atrium. The others are closed behind metal doors, utilitarian, fire escapes.

There is one of these next to the bathroom Morgan has come out of, so she is climbing it, slowing to a tiptoe when she hears voices above, a man's and a woman's— quiet voices like those of people with a secret. She has already heard them, would already be embarrassed for them to know it, and she hides, pressed against a wall waiting for them to leave so she can pass.

"Why'd you bother coming today?" the man is asking. "Save it for when the Finnemore trial starts."

"Finnemore is taking forever."

The man is Joshua Lund. And the woman is probably, hopefully, his wife, the one Morgan remembers seeing him with at the restaurant.

"And it's too hilarious, seeing you in this fancy get-up," the woman goes on. "Un-scariest baby brother Grim Reaper ever. How could I miss the chance to come to court on a Grim Reaper day?"

"Fine," he says. "But same courthouse rules as always. Nothing brotherly. Don't act like we're connected. And make sure no one follows you to your car on the way out."

"Joshua, you're not the boss of me," she says. "And you can bet everyone here who has a personal history with your arsonist knows better than we do how badly he needs to be locked up for some rehab. No one is going to be mad at you for getting the job done. No one's going to try to take it out on your family."

"Probably, but—look Gigi, everyone on trial here suffers from impulse control problems and terrible judgment. Unpredictable bad behaviour—that's the one thing we can count on here. So keep a low profile. You never know."

He leaves the stairwell first, turning to speak to her over his shoulder. "Don't follow right after me. *Deng yi xia*."

She—the woman Morgan now knows is the prosecutor's sister—doesn't wait long before heading to the courtroom. Morgan is close behind her, gliding through the door before it can close. The woman, the sister, is the same person as the one from the restaurant. She doesn't sit in the half of the gallery behind the prosecutor's desk— the bride's side, as Tod calls it. Instead, she sits behind the arsonist's aunties or fairy godmothers or whoever they are—the ladies on the groom's side of the courtroom.

Nothing is happening—not really. This is the face of court Morgan knows best—its bored, yawning, waiting face. There is a clerk behind a desk, dressed in a black robe, stacking and unstacking papers, snapping rubber bands. Lawyers come in, making clunky bows at the bar, stepping up to the counsel desks. The arsonist's lawyer isn't ready to go ahead, so other lawyers are using the sitting judge's time to set their own matters over. The same, always the same.

The judge is a man a bit older than Morgan's father but much richer, fat and fancy, his black robes encircled by a red sash. When he comes into the room, everyone is ordered to rise and wait while he takes his seat under a bronze coat of arms. He is short enough that his black silk robe fits him like a garbage-bag rain poncho.

Courtrooms don't have windows. They have carpet and upholstery, polished wood, microphones that record but don't amplify. Carpeting runs up the walls, and dusty beige drapes meant to baffle the noise of the common people sitting in the gallery hang from the ceiling overhead, like tea towels pinned to a clothesline.

Morgan sits straining to hear the judge and the lawyers through a wool blanket wound around her head. It's not really made of wool. It's not really a blanket, just the heaviness of the pauses, a thickness of the courtroom air made partly of boredom, partly of impatience and nerves—her own and everyone else's.

The pre-show of setting matters over does not last all morning. Eventually, the NCR arson trial begins, and Joshua Lund stands and reads an Agreed Statement of Facts. Yes, yes, this man admits he is the one who used bolt-cutters to break through a chain-link fence, stole the office's petty cash box, tossed around an open gas can, lit enough of it to set seven RVs on fire, and fled on a jacked quad. Yes, yes, he was ranting and distraught when the police found him stuck in a snowbank. But look—just look at these photos of his injuries, his hands and arms magnified larger than life-sized, set on easels in high resolution colour at the front of the courtroom. Yes, those are a living human being's arms—purpled-red as if they've been flayed, oozing with plasma. Anyone in his right mind would be crazy, inconsolable upon immolating his own arms for two hundred dollars in cash, some fireworks, and a joy ride. That's not a sign of a disease of the mind. That's grief, that's humanity. Nothing is more sane.

Morgan leans against the back of the gallery bench, away from the photos. The dry wood beneath her creaks in the quiet. She bends over her knees, bracing her hands against the edge of her seat, touching the bottom of it where someone has left a wad of gum as a protest, sticking it to the court system the best way they could. The handprints smeared on the courthouse's glass doors and walls, the unflushed toilets in the bathrooms—all of it is protest.

Hours may pass before anyone moves for a recess for lunch. Morgan feels weak, but she doesn't want to eat. She wants air. There is nothing left to breathe, no space left between her face and the wool blanket around her head. There are three ways to escape the blanket: throwing up, passing out, or rising up and walking away. All three are impossible.

No, she stands up, holding onto the back of the bench in front of her as if it's a handrail, the soles of her shoes snagging along the carpet of the aisle, moving toward the doors, so slowly.

Voices drone behind her, to the judge: "M'Lord, M'Lord…"

She has reached the back of the room. There is a space, a gap between the last of the benches and the handles of the doors. If she goes any farther, there will be nothing to hold on to for an instant. She can't keep standing here, so she lets go, hoping there is enough air in the empty space to keep her afloat until she finds the next handhold.

There is not.

Morgan hears her own voice speaking, saying something about fainting in public.

Someone answers. "You went one better than that. You fainted on the public record."

Above her is the woman from the restaurant, Gillian Lund, the tips of her hair dangling toward Morgan's face. Beyond Gillian's head, Morgan sees a smooth white ceiling trimmed with yellowing golden oak. They are in the hallway outside the courtroom, Morgan's head in Gillian's lap, her feet far away as she lies stretched across two concrete cubes topped with purple upholstery, like tuffets set together in a row. This woman and Morgan are touching, their bodies in contact, kept barely apart by their clothing. The back of Morgan's cranium rests on the flesh over Gillian's femurs. This woman is the prosecutor's secret sister, the patron saint of strangers who pass out in public.

Morgan closes her eyes, groans something about being a baby.

"No, you're not a baby. Believe me," Gillian says. "Believe Auntie Gigi, there is no way a baby would have gone that quietly."

Morgan is raising herself onto her elbows, breaking their touch. But then Gillian is bracing Morgan's shoulders with one of her arms, its heat spanning Morgan's back. "Easy, slowly. Don't be embarrassed about lying down out here. There's always somebody doing it."

Morgan is sitting, bearing her own weight, but bent at the waist, her head over her knees. Gillian lets her arm fall away. They must have stopped court to get Morgan out of the room.

"Just for a few minutes," Gillian says. "Don't worry

about it. The sheriffs live for that kind of drama. I think they enjoy it more when the person being carried out of the courtroom puts up a fight, though. They got you out of there pretty fast. I'm not sure the lawyers even noticed." It's a joke. She proves it by laughing. Her voice is loud, like a nurse coming into a hospital room.

Morgan glances at the closed courtroom doors, groans again, lowering her face into her hands.

Gillian pats her back, touching Morgan with her palm and the inner surfaces of her fingers. "Every human faints. My brave brother almost lost it the last time he had a routine blood test—thought he heard something gurgling in the tubing. And who can blame you for being woozy? Those photo exhibits of the burn injuries were nasty."

Morgan wants to accept it—all of it—grace after grace.

Gillian is still talking, introducing herself by name. "So, you don't really know me, and this is going to sound creepy as frick, but I think I know you. You're a family member of the Finnemore homicide victim, right?"

This, Morgan now knows, is what they call her—Gillian, her brother, everyone in this courthouse. She is Family Member of the Finnemore Victim. Of course she is.

Morgan swallows, nods.

"Right. Morgan Turner." She starts as Gillian pronounces her real name. Gillian sees and says, "I've been following the Finnemore case since the very beginning. I'm a graduate student, and criminal law transcripts are part of my research. I guess I picked up on your name. I'm just a member of the public but I'm familiar with the case and it's—so awful. I'm not a stalker—which, I know is something only a stalker would have to say but—I'm just—just really touched by what happened. I'm so sorry."

Gillian waits, lets the water settle and clear around them, disturbs it again. "I've seen your parents on television. And someone—someone who works here—pointed you out to me once, at your restaurant, during your shift. There's no reason for you to remember. We didn't speak to each other but I saw you. Dang, that sounds creepy."

This space made for waiting outside the courtrooms on the third floor, this place where strangers have handled Morgan's body, one of them staying behind to touch her head and back and call her by name—this is a place for moments of truth. This is where people tell horrible secrets, whispering to each other in the carpeted closeness, scared, about to pass into courtrooms where they will try to either come clean or perfect a deceit. In this place, Morgan could ask Gillian Lund anything. She could ask her what she and her brother have said about "the family" all those times the Finnemore victim was mentioned. She could ask how someone like Gillian came to spend her days touching and being touched by her brother, by the babies who call her Auntie, by strangers, whoever she wants.

Instead, Morgan blurts the words 'negatively identified' fast and hard as if she's vomiting on her shoes. She wants to know if there can be any such thing as negatively identified human remains.

Gillian tilts her head gently enough to keep her dizziness away but conspicuously enough to signal careful consideration. "Negatively identified?"

Morgan tries again, more slowly, explaining how, at the beginning, when they first found Tricia, the police said female remains had been positively identified as hers.

Gillian gets it. "Police officers have their own idiolect. Think of it as linguistic body armour. Let them have it. It's nothing."

Morgan's shoulders are slumping. Nothing—it can't be nothing.

Gillian sees. "Negatively identified," she repeats. "Let's try harder. Okay, I guess it could be possible, but not easy, to negatively identify someone. What you'd have to do is line up every female living on the planet— every candidate to become female human remains. And then, after you'd seen them all and determined none of the living females was your sister, you could be sure the unnamed remains would have to be hers."

Morgan is considering it as the doors of the courtroom open. The judge has already ordered an early break for lunch to clear everyone's head after the commotion of a member of the public passing out in the gallery. People disperse into offices and bathrooms, to the patios outside for cigarettes.

Gillian glances at Joshua as he strides past their tuffets in his black robes. He might be unhappy with her. Running to the rescue of a fainting girl during open court is not a low-profile operation.

When he is gone from sight, Gillian scans the waiting area. "Whoa." She gasps, flushing pink, smiling in a way Morgan hasn't seen yet. "Uh-oh. Excuse me, Morgan Turner. Sit tight. Don't try to walk away yet."

Gillian has stood up and called to someone waiting beside the doors of a docket courtroom. "Dana Randall! Dana, oh my gosh! Look at you!"

The woman Gillian has crossed the room to gush over is a lady about her own age. She looks like a lawyer, one dressed in a tight suit that must have fit better when she bought it—though Morgan wouldn't have noticed if Gillian hadn't ordered everyone who could hear to look. The lady is not smiling, even as Gillian rushes toward her with all of her teeth bared in a grin. "Dana, look at you. I hadn't heard you're expecting again! Look at that belly. It's adorable. You must be six months along already. Wow, I am so happy for you—and for Mitch too. All the best to you guys, from Josh and me."

Dana Randall straightens her jacket, sucks in her breath so her body shifts beneath her clothes. She folds her arms in front of herself, lowers her chin. She does look like she might be pregnant, but not enough to keep the prospect of commenting on it from being terrifying, foolhardy—cruel.

She says something vulgar—something strange—about Gillian being Josh's sister-wife before she turns and shoulders through the doors of the docket courtroom.

Gillian Lund has never had any intention of keeping a low profile. She is laughing—laughing so loudly a sheriff peeks out of a doorway to assess the risk of it. She hushes at the sight of him, sitting down next to Morgan, apologizing, pawing through her bag for Kleenex. "Wow, that was vile. But so worth it. What was she so mad about though, eh? There's no shame in having a healthy round belly, right? Oh my heck. Can you believe the mouth on that girl?" She is still laughing. "Now you know, Morgan Turner. I am not actually a good person. Dana Randall is not good either but that's no excuse. Ho, no. I know better."

She glances at the closed docket courtroom doors and laughs all over again. Dana Randall is not pregnant. By now, even Morgan knows it.

"No, not at all," Gillian admits. "Aren't I awful? She and her husband are both former colleagues of—of my brother's. They hated him, thought he was getting assignments they deserved, standing in the way of their brilliant legal careers. So they went scheming and complaining instead of doing any work." She refolds her Kleenex, stashing it for later. "I've got to let it go. Personally, I hardly know them—met them at couple times at fakey-fake work barbeques and that's it. The happy couple works somewhere else now anyways."

Morgan asks a question she knows the answer for, testing to see if it will be kept from her. She asks if Gillian's brother is a prosecutor here.

Gillian coughs. "What? Sure. Hey, how's your head feeling?"

"Gillian! I thought I saw you in there." Someone is straggling late out of Joshua Lund's courtroom, another Department of Justice employee calling across the waiting area.

Gillian stands up, waving both her hands. "Shh. No one's supposed to know me. Josh said he didn't—"

Gillian's courthouse friend rolls her eyes. "Josh needs to get over himself. Come eat with us, we're down in the cafeteria."

Hoisting her purse onto her shoulder, Gillian pins her hair beneath the strap. She tries to flip it free, tearing and splitting her hair. "Nice to meet you, Morgan—well, nice for me, anyways. Sorry you're not feeling well." Gillian pats Morgan's shoulder one more time. "Don't get up too fast, okay? Find some juice and drink it before you leave. And you'd better get checked out by a doctor. Alright?"

Morgan nods, bows her head into her fingertips. Looking down, she can see Gillian's feet, her brown leather shoes, still stained with wavy white lines from winter's road salt, standing a half-taken step away.

"I can't," Gillian says, the feet turning. "I can't leave you like this, not Morgan Turner. Let's find a walk-in clinic and get you checked out."

Morgan argues. She's fine. There's a bus outside every ten minutes. It's fine.

Gillian mutters something about "fatherless and widows," and they are outside in the parking lot. She drives Morgan to a storefront clinic, registers her at the reception desk, and checks the time on her phone. She winces. "I can't stay any longer," she says. "Stupid theory class—promise me you won't go home until you've seen the doctor."

Morgan's head wobbles in something like a nod.

"Here." Gillian has extracted a scrap of cardstock from

the bottom of her bag, spilling library checkout receipts and pens onto the floor. She is writing on the back of the card. "You and me—we are friends now. I have seen you unconscious, and it's too late to go back to being strangers. And your first act of friendship to me is going to be to text me to let me know how things go with the doctor. I need to know. So here's my number."

Morgan takes the card, reads the string of digits written on it in ink. Outside, Gillian is already waving through the windshield of her car as she backs into traffic. Morgan sits in the waiting room of the clinic, fingering the card, flipping it to the printed side, the one marked with the logo for the Department of Justice, and the name of Finnemore's prosecutor.

7

Morgan intended to stay at the clinic for the three hours it would take to see a doctor. She intended to send Gillian Lund a short, warm text to report on her continued good health. And she would have succeeded in her first act of friendship if the Freibergs human resources department hadn't called her, there in the clinic's waiting room, to tease Morgan with a confession of its love. Freibergs was falling for Morgan's food service skills—her soggy, steamy, stupid food service skills. Their two o'clock job interview had cancelled. If she could come right away, the interview slot would be hers.

She pumped disinfectant gel into her palms and walked out of the clinic to find a bus. Later that afternoon, she left the factory a probationary Freibergs employee. An entire family of migrant workers has just quit to move to Vancouver. Freibergs, in its moment of desperation, had taken up with Morgan Turner.

At home, Tod learns she has defied him and found a job at the abattoir. "I don't get it, Morgo. What do you want from there? You want to be grossed out, traumatized, scarred for life?"

Sheila shouts him down from where she stands, still in her nursing scrubs, scramble-frying ground beef in the kitchen. "What do you mean, what does she want? It's a factory job, her first one with good union benefits. It's obvious what she wants from it."

Tod won't have it. "No, it's not just that. It's the scalder, isn't it? She's got a thing about the scalder. It's morbid. You're trying to go goth. You're emo now, aren't you Morgo?"

If she is, it has already been frustrated. Her new position is not in Tod's horror movie but in a clean well-lit room somewhere near it. The room is Freibergs's employee cafeteria. It has a large commercial dishwasher for her to operate—one that makes the clean dishes so hot Morgan believes they are melting her fingerprints away. That's got to be a bit horrifying. The machine is probably a lot like Tod's hog scalder, only it's not for dead animals but for coffee mugs and soup bowls.

"No, it's not a thing like the scalder," Tod tells her as they drive home after her first day of work. "The scalder is a heavy-duty, stainless steel industrial food processing system—long and deep as a full-grown man. We slam the hog inside and blast its hide bald before it heads down the line for evisceration. I'd like to see your dishwasher do that."

At least he is making conversation with her. Morgan's world has become quieter now that she has left the friendliness of the fast food restaurant kitchen. Vincenta and the rest of the ladies would sing and hug at work. The ladies in the Freibergs kitchen are different. They are immigrant workers, like most of the old restaurant crew. But they are not from the Philippines, and they're certainly not Spanish. Morgan doesn't want to jump to ignorant conclusions, but she is fairly sure they are from China itself. Their English is correct but difficult, and Morgan can't make out even a single word of what they say to each other in Chinese, not even what they're calling each other when they use their real names instead of the English ones they drew out of their school teachers' fists, like lots— Lilian, Melanie, Anita, Phoenix.

It is lonely, austerely sanitary, but the abattoir cafeteria is still the most highbrow place Morgan has ever worked. Weeks pass, and it becomes almost fun sometimes, in the middle of the afternoon when the lunch rush and mess are over, and the Freibergs cafeteria ladies sit down and watch television while they eat their own meals. Television time is when Morgan and the rest of the staff begin to connect, sitting still, saying almost nothing. They show her soap operas—not American ones, and not the gritty British melodramas that have played on the CBC every day of Morgan's life. The cafeteria ladies watch shows where the people all look Chinese to Morgan, but can't be. If they were Chinese, she reasons, the ladies would be able to understand what the actors were saying without reading the dialogue from subtitles printed on the bottom of the screen in characters. Above the characters, printed in a different colour, are English subtitles for Morgan. The ladies don't have to play versions of their shows uploaded with this English, but they do.

The subtitles mention Seoul enough times that Morgan figures out the language and the actors are Korean—beautifully, eerily perfect South Korean actors, models, and singers. The subtitlers are amateurs, translating as literally as possible, leaving the idioms in their original, sometimes jarring forms—young male leads playfully asking their onscreen girlfriends if they want to die. The language seems impossible at first but Morgan starts to recognize bits of it—important, plot-propelling expressions characters scream at each other in the streets. She thinks *saranghae* is Korean for "I love you," *mianhae* means "I'm sorry," and *kajima* means "don't go."

It all means Morgan is annoyed when Tod barges into the Freibergs dining room at TV time. "Come on, Morgo."

The cafeteria ladies look up from their lunchboxes, and Morgan sees Tod as they do. They haven't met him before—big Tod Turner who eats alone in his car, trying to read his book. Tod's weight is not something Morgan takes personally. He doesn't mind his size and neither does she. What she does mind, what she learned to shrink from when she was still a kid, is the possibility of anyone mistaking her for being related to him by romance instead of by blood. Sister, sister—she is not his wife or girlfriend, but his sister. It is an ongoing misunderstanding for brothers and sisters born close together, looking nothing alike. She doesn't laugh it off, like Gillian Lund. Morgan rushes at the assumption, tackling it into the turf. She does it even though she knows to speak against it too forcefully is to say too much—to draw attention to the empty space where her love and sex-life ought to be.

When she comes back to the kitchen after her errand with Tod, maybe she will find the nerve to ask the ladies to teach her the Chinese word for brother. Until then, she explains nothing. She crams the crust of her sandwich into her mouth and stands up beside Tod.

The tables in the cafeteria are filling with employees from the floor, scuffing the clean tiles with steel-toed gum boots, pawing at the hot coffee mugs Morgan had just finished stacking before her lunch. The entire factory is taking a break at the same time.

"Shut down," Tod explains as he walks ahead of her, fingering keypads, shoving doors aside. "We're down for maintenance for the next half hour. Happens once a month. Everyone who's not working like crazy to get us running again has nothing to do for a little while. So if you're interested in seeing the scalder, now is the time."

He stops walking when he no longer hears the sound of Morgan's footsteps on the floor behind him. "Look, I blame myself," Tod says over his shoulder. "I shouldn't have told you anything about the scalder. I should have known you'd get weird about it. It's basically just an industrial shower cabinet for dead things. It's—no." Tod looks away from her, shakes his head. "It's just a dumb machine. Come see for yourself."

Morgan follows, the cafeteria smells—the coffee and boiling canola oil—fading away as the air gets wetter. The processing floor smells like rubber and bleach, and beneath that, barnyards—hog barnyards with a stench like the feces of something fed on vomit, or the vomit of something fed on feces.

"Some of the guys have tried to call the scalder 'she' and give it a human name and everything," Tod says. "But nothing sticks. The scalder is just the scalder."

Over their heads, the fiberglass tiles of the false ceiling are gone and the underside of the factory's steel roof is bared. The lights above are kettle drums mounted upside down, sealed, and burning with something too bright to look at. Not everything is shut down. The space is noisy with refrigeration compressors. Hung low enough for Tod to reach it is a bar like a heavy gauge curtain rod. It follows the path they are traveling. Chains hang down from the bar and on the end of each chain is a metal clamp bent into a loop.

There they are, a line of hog carcasses hanging from the rod, each of them caught by one hind hoof snared in a metal loop as if it's a trap the animal has stumbled into—as if the hogs weren't bred and born for no other purpose than to be hanging here. Ears, snouts, eyes, everything—it's all still in the hogs' faces. The throats have been stuck, wounds rimmed red with fresh, watery blood Morgan can smell before she can see it.

Scoff at anyone who says girls are scared of blood, even thick, black, clotted blood. Most of the time, all blood means to a girl is that everything is exactly as it should be. Abattoir blood doesn't smell like Morgan's healthy, human blood. It is diluted, cold, with a pH made too basic by all the bleach. It's not good blood but it isn't quite scary either—not like the effects spattered in movies, not like the red ooze of burnt arsonist arms.

When maintenance is over and the plant is back in production, Tod will guide these huge, pink-white bodies into the scalder, one by one. He walks the line of dead, inverted hogs. With a girth as wide as his, Tod can't help but brush against them with one shoulder. They bob out of his way before they drift back into Morgan's path, bumping against her like big, cold, docile dogs—oblivious, harmless.

Tod has stopped beside a steel table bolted to a concrete floor that never fully dries. The table is like the kind actors in crime shows on American television stand around while they pretend to do autopsies on other actors, painted grey, who are good at holding their breaths and staring. Right now, the table is empty.

Tod pulls a blue, rubber apron over his head, like Morgan always imagined he would. He waves across the table. "That's it there, Morgo."

The scalder—it is a rounded box about as long as Tod is tall. It is lying horizontally, mounted on legs so it opens at Tod's waist height. It's like a stainless-steel coffin set on a bier. Tod grasps a handle and raises its lid. "Opens up here, hog goes in, shut the lid, wait, hog comes out, goes down the line to evisceration. That's it," Tod says. "That's it for now, anyways. They don't make scalders like this anymore. Most of the plants are switching over to big cabinet systems—no more manual singeing and loading, just hogs on hooks, moving smooth and uninterrupted on down the line. It's only a matter of time before Freibergs upgrades too."

Morgan touches the lid of the scalder with her fingertips. The metal is wet but not warm anymore.

There is a blaring buzz and a grind. The line of straps on the curtain rod lurches forward and then lapses back, blood trickling from slit throats onto the wet floors.

"We're up," Tod says.

The maintenance break is over. The carcasses are moving again, but not quickly enough. Tod is dragging a hog by its forefoot toward the table. He doesn't use a hook, just his hand. An electric pulley lowers the hog to the tabletop where Tod singes it with the blue flame from a torch. When he's done, the pulley raises the carcass high enough for him to swing it into the scalder. There's a roar as the cylinder fills with steam and hot water. It overflows, wetting the floor—pink juices Tod blasts with a hose until they disappear into the drain.

The scalder shimmies as the brushes and rollers inside it whip the hair out of the hog's hide. It only lasts a minute or two. The scalder is open, the clean, hairless hog is slipped back into its foot-trap and hoisted into the line. Tod begins again.

He calls to his sister over the racket of his manually loaded scalder, his dying craft. "Okay, Morgo? Back to the dish-pit?"

She leaves. She leaves like any new initiate, considering something that was much less and much more than expected, all at once. Going back to the cafeteria, getting out, there are no locks on her side of the doors.

8

Never make an idle comment about chronic vertigo to an old friend who has grown up to become a neurologist. Gillian learned this during dinner party small talk with Dr. Jeff. She triggered his pathological fastidiousness, a trait he might medicate as an anxiety disorder in other people but one he values highly in himself, a trait that got him into and then out the other side of medical school, one that keeps him always a little bit at work. Dr. Jeff is a medical incarnation of Josh. They are noble professionals, today's knightly class—righteousness, diligence, pride, and overkill.

Gillian moved her head too quickly when she turned to speak to Jeff, and the dinner party became awkward as only a doctor-knight can make it. Her spoon was still in her hand, but her head was cradled between the tips of all ten of his fingers, tipping and rolling. Jeff's wife sat on the other side of him, leaning forward to watch, laughing, apologizing. His face was close enough to Gillian's over their dessert bowls that she could only shut her eyes and laugh along.

"Seriously, Jeff?"

"I don't like it, Gill," he said. "I do not like it at all. You hit your head on something?"

"No, nothing unusual."

"You take an iron supplement?"

"Sick. That's for pregnant ladies."

"No, I don't like it. Open your eyes and look up into the light."

She blinked into the burning filaments of their hosts' brushed nickel chandelier. "My family doctor says it's a harmless nuisance. He said not to worry and taught me this therapeutic turning maneuver that makes me want to puke like I've been on a roller coaster."

Jeff hummed. "The overwhelming odds are that he's right. But we've got a study on paroxysmal vertigo underway at the University Hospital. It's a bit late but I'm signing you up. You'll be getting a call."

That is how Gillian came to be stripped down to a hospital gown, her back on a table, her head in a spongy tray, her face covered by a metal cage the technicians call a helmet.

"Like astronauts wear."

But there is no space here. Gillian's head is in the centre of a small ring. Her ears are covered, but she can hear the bang, crash and buzz from behind the smooth, white walls of the narrow chamber. She is having an MRI scan— painless, non-invasive. The racket inside the machine has been the most shocking thing about the procedure. The chamber doesn't spin or shift. It would be less worrisome if it did—if she could see the source of the noise, connect it to a visible, mechanical narrative like every living person wants to do when we run to a window when something crashes outside. Un-seeable, the noise brings a sense of blindness, obstruction, of lying in a closed casket, the heavy municipal machinery arriving to finish the burial.

Gillian's task is to lie still in the white light and not succumb to claustrophobic panic. She twitches, regretting her brave but silly refusal of the Ativan she was offered to calm her nerves before the test started. Stupid. She needs to think of something deeply compelling, distracting. There it is. She has found it here in the scanner, where it must have been left by thousands of patients before her. Gillian will think of the only thing there is to consider in a place so clean and small. She will think about what would become of her loved ones if anything happened to her—if Dr. Jeff does indeed diagnose her with a catastrophic neurological glitch and she dies, not in fifty years, after she's got her doctorate and maybe a decent husband and some kids, but soon.

People who share their everyday lives discuss these questions together. People like Gillian, who go through their days more or less independent of anyone else, look around their apartments, at their cats' guileless but carnivorous faces, and wonder what would happen—afterwards. Gillian Lund does not have a cat.

In the MRI chamber, the technician has come to shift Gillian's body, pressing her through her gown, adjusting her position in the scanner. Through the earpieces, they tell her the test is half over.

Without a cat, the practical problems, the daily inconveniences brought on by Gillian's death would be most problematic for Paul—Paulie whom she adores but will not allow to move into her apartment with her, whom she could not recommend as a partner to anyone else, not right now. When she dies, Paul will have no one to watch over him but the always unavailable Joshua. Paul would come to her untimely funeral, cry, tear at his hangnails, wonder what comet flew overhead, what space helmet she must have failed to wear to protect the atoms in her brain from disruption, from spinning to death. He would leave the chapel marking the days until the same thing was bound to happen to himself. Himself—always at the beginning and the end of every manic delusion—himself. But the death-comet would not come for him and he would go on in a post-Gillian world. Slowly, things would fall apart around him—things he has never acknowledged her for holding together.

Paul made a rare phone call to Gillian's house last Sunday night. He only ever calls with what he imagines is terrible news. "Gillian, I fed some pigeons and now I'm pretty sure I have bird flu." "Gillian, someone phoned my answering machine and yelled at me about some paperwork I never heard of. I'm going to be homeless now, aren't I?"

This time, he had truly bad news. Josh had forgotten to turn the ringer of his phone back on again, so he was calling Gillian, asking her to find their brother and bring him to meet in person to talk. They gathered in a coffee shop far enough from Paul's place for it not to be too seedy. Josh bought him a Coke and a ludicrously expensive café brownie, and they braced for impact.

"Yeah, so I forgot to go to the counselling the court ordered with my mental health diversion, and now I've been charged with failure to obey a court order."

Josh made an awful face. "What? You knew you had counselling to do, didn't you?"

"Well, yeah."

"And you decided not to go?"

"Decided—no, of course not. I forgot about it. I just—forgot. It's my meds. They wreck my short term memory."

"But you know to expect that. The doctor explained that to you. They gave you strategies. You have ways to deal with your bad memory, don't you? You wrote your counselling appointments down, didn't you?"

"Yeah, but then I forgot to look at my calendar."

"How—"

Gillian crumpled her napkin, threw it onto the table. "Josh, stop cross-examining him. It doesn't help. It's done."

All those pat-downs at the courthouse security station, the letters, meetings, Gillian's hand on his back as he wept in the courtroom gallery—it's nothing, gone. The hours of paper and legwork, the triumph of weathering the crisis without getting a criminal record—it disappeared into the darkness of Paul's brain.

Gillian was furious—with Paul, with the probation

officer who was supposed to be supervising him, with herself for not realizing he could let something so simple and vital slip away. But fury would have had no meaning. She laid her head on the café table and laughed. "Admit it," she said. "It's time you admit it, Paulie. You've always wanted to go to jail. You're dying to go to jail. You must be."

He laughed back at her.

She said, "You want to see jail from the inside, as research for a fabulous, gritty, alienated white-boy novel you've been secretly writing this whole time. I can't wait to read it. It'd better be good. The climactic scene will be all about courtroom drama, where you're convicted but still able to strut nobly out of the prisoner's dock, all the way to jail."

"What? No," Paul said. "Come on. In my book, the climactic scene is where I fall in love."

"In jail."

"He is not going to jail," Josh interrupted. "He is going to plead guilty—because he is guilty. He is going to get the criminal record he's worked so hard for, get fined a few hundred dollars, and then register in a programme where he does community service until the fine is worked off."

Paul raked his fingers through his hair, frowned for the first time that evening. "Community service."

Gillian sang, "Breakin' rocks…"

Josh sneered. "More like picking up garbage, or scraping gum off the bottoms of the picnic tables on Churchill Square."

At the paroxysmal positional vertigo study, the radiography technician is back in the MRI room. "Okay, Gillian, all done."

The table slides free of the scanner, away from the grip of the helmet. The moment she can, Gillian bolts to sitting. The room spins around her, crashes sideways with force enough to make her ears ring.

The technician sees and takes her by the arm. "That vertigo is no joke, eh?"

Gillian tries to laugh anyway. "Are we really done? Can I go home? They don't want me to come back upstairs so they can shine more lights in my eyes, do they? It sounds painless but to tell you the truth, at this point I'd rather get a big needle than have another blinding light beamed into in my eyes."

She has just finished saying it when she realizes she is about to get both.

9

Morgan Turner is not a good friend. She is pleasant, but not friendly. Consuming someone else's time and space—even that of people required by blood to abide her—seems like an imposition, impossible. She had friends in school, when she was a child—"little friends," Tod had called them. Truly enough, they were her friends only a very little.

Odd, accidental friendships are the best fits for Morgan—unlikely friendships assembled through the trickery of propinquity, through sheer time spent stuck in the same room with someone. Morgan's best friend is not Gillian Lund, who saw her unconscious, declared that they can never again be strangers, but hasn't seen her in nearly a year. Gillian Lund came into the pestilence of the walk-in clinic's waiting room with her, expressing Morgan's manifest destiny, a unilateral declaration of friendship Morgan had wanted to be true. Maybe the phone call from Freibergs that drew her out of the clinic, out of the way of Gillian Lund, was a cosmic mercy—an escape hatch sparing Gillian from the burden of friendship with Morgan. That's how Morgan excused herself for not calling. Grace enough to spare her from being Morgan's friend—Gillian must deserve it.

In truth, Morgan's best friend is, as usual, a coworker she is formally scheduled by forces beyond either of their control to see on a daily basis. The woman is a fellow Freibergs kitchen lady. Morgan can barely converse with her, and she might be closer to Sheila's age than to hers, for all Morgan knows. She told Morgan to call her Lilian— the same thing the plant services manager calls her, which none of the other kitchen ladies calls her.

Lilian studied English as part of her state education in China. She speaks it far better than Morgan will ever, ever speak Chinese. Every member of the cafeteria staff does. They use English with the workers from the floor—with the men reeking of rubber and isopropyl alcohol hand sanitizer—but when breaks are over and the kitchen ladies have the cafeteria to themselves, they set their second language aside. It isn't because they don't like Morgan, but because they do. They understand her and are able to make themselves understood by her without much English, as if they are characters in a *Star Wars* movie, calling and answering in different languages, content enough with the sense they can make of each other. Almost a year into her Freibergs career, it is not the Chinese language Morgan understands. It is the ladies themselves, Lilian in particular.

The talk between them is not deep or complicated or even interesting. Their conversations are short and follow a simple structure—consistent, low-risk, perfect. Morgan will ask Lilian how to say the names of things in Chinese,

Lilian will tell her, Morgan will repeat them all wrong, and everyone will laugh.

"Laughter of encouragement," Lilian says. "Just encouragement."

If she had been experimenting with Chinese vocabulary out of idle curiosity, Morgan never would have broached the barrier, the great wall of the other kitchen ladies' first language. But she was provoked. She didn't ask them the Chinese word for brother the day Tod called her out of the kitchen to see the scalder. It was the everyday routine of sitting with the ladies, watching them eat their lunches out of plastic boxes, picking at rice and long green vegetables with chopsticks, that finally pushed her out of her quiet. "Chopstick" is a word the police and the lawyers and Finnemore's confession video use. It's no good. Morgan needed to learn to think of the ordinary chopsticks in the ladies' lunches as something else, index them inside her mind by a word no one she had met at the courthouse would know.

She spoke to the ladies conversationally rather than functionally for the first time, asking them how to say chopsticks in Chinese.

At first, no one said anything in any language. The room went quiet. Morgan's face flushed with blood.

Lilian was the one who answered. "筷子."

One hearing of a new Chinese word is never enough. Morgan tried to repeat it anyway.

The ladies laughed behind their hands. Lilian waved them quiet. "Good," she said to Morgan. She pointed at her own pair of chopsticks with her free hand. "But not 'kwide-suh.' No, no. 筷子, 筷子."

Morgan can't write any of her new vocabulary down, and the words tend to sound too much alike for her to keep them from breaking into static inside her brain. Only a few words and phrases stand out. 你干嘛 means something like "what the heck are you doing?" and 为什么 is "why." The longer a word is, the easier it is for her to tell it apart from the rest of the noise and understand it. She knows only a few short words. Eventually, she learned that Tod is her 哥, and that the pigs at the factory are 猪子, a word with a first syllable that sounds a lot like "Jew" to Morgan. Another great wall—Morgan remembers the word but will never be able to use it.

It is early, early in the spring when the ladies from the cafeteria first convince Morgan they would like to spend time with her outside of work. She will join them at a festival with a name Morgan doesn't remember—a Chinese holiday they don't usually bother to mention to foreigners. Lilian tells Morgan to dress to be outdoors and meet them at a train station at noon.

By now, Morgan has watched enough East Asian television to feel like it would be coarse of her to arrive as Lilian's guest without a small gift.

"How should I know what the cafeteria ladies would like, Morgo?" Tod said. "Get some weird Asian fruit— like those gigantic greenish grapefruit-looking things, so you don't come across as too ignorant."

Pomelos—he meant pomelos, and Morgan knows she won't find any at the Safeway. She rides the bus downtown, almost all the way to the river, a slow, straight route along 97 Street, parallel to the blocks of soup kitchens where the city gets rough. It is an area known for sunburnt, strung out pedestrian traffic, some of which winds up on the bus—noisy, smelly, scary. Morgan sits pressed to a dirty window, turned away from the man waving his arms and talking to everyone, as if they are a congregation gathered at his feet.

"Lo and behold, thus saith the Lord!"

She can hear and smell him but she can't be made to see him. The end of the world—why is public ranting always apocalyptic? Maybe she should take some of the sweet union wages Freibergs has been paying her and buy a car, one with no one in it but her. She could drive it somewhere, park it, eat some food in it.

She disembarks at the red gate spanning the street, marking the entrance to the city's Chinatown. There is writing on it—gold-coloured aluminum bent and moulded into the shapes of brush strokes, unreadable to her, a secret code shared by a billion people.

Golden Grocery sits on the eastern side of the road, the door flanked by lions cast out of concrete, guardians of the building and the people inside. The guardians might promise Morgan safety but they can't promise her pomelos. She doesn't find any, circles the produce department a second time, and hears something strange in this place: loud conversational English.

"All girls want," a man is saying, "is someone who won't cheat on them. They don't care about anything else."

A woman laughs. "Bro, seriously? Who told you that?"

Morgan turns toward the sound of English like a compass swiveling north. One of the Anglo voices belongs to a man who looks at home here on 97 Street—lanky, rough, and hairy. The other voice belongs to Gillian Lund. She hasn't seen Morgan yet when she shoves the man, scoffing. "Seriously, Paulie, who told you that? Have you started hanging out with the soup kitchen lunatics again?"

"No."

"Well, good!" she stops in the middle of the produce department, folds her arms and asks no one and everyone, "What happened to all the pomelos in this town? I've looked everywhere."

The man moves away from the centre of the floor, backs into a table of onions in mesh bags. "Just forget it then. What do we need pomelos for? What does anyone need them for?"

She smirks. "It's that thing again—that festival Josh likes to celebrate now that Chinese New Year has gone all mainstream. I asked dear sister-in-law if I could bring anything to their picnic and she said pomelos."

"Josh—maybe it's time he got over the whole Chinese thing."

"What? Time to get over his mission? *Tu plaisantes!* Of course it's not. People don't get over their missions. I never got over mine."

He whistles, onion skins crinkling as he pushes himself away from the produce table. "I sure didn't get over mine either."

"Maybe, you did. Maybe that's your problem. No, what Josh does have to get over are pomelos. They're impossible to find in Edmonton half the year, and they're nothing but grapefruit with too much peel anyways, and I've—"

Morgan has been spotted.

Gillian interrupts herself, trots across the produce department, takes Morgan by the arm. She is looking into each of Morgan's pupils in turn, the way Dr. Jeff looks into hers. "Morgan! Morgan Turner—honey, are you okay? Are you better now? I should have punched my number right into your phone before I dumped you there at that clinic and took off. Sorry."

Morgan smiles at her shoes, tries to laugh. She is fine, apologizing, explaining about the sudden job opportunity at Freibergs, how busy it's made her.

"Well, no wonder I never saw you at that restaurant ever again. Never mind being sorry, just be okay. Are you okay? Honestly, I was this close to searching the past year's worth of obituaries, looking for you." There is a resilience in Gillian's affection—a willful insensibility to slights and burdens. She is like something from the Bible about bearing all things, hoping all things, enduring all things—clambering over offenses, hanging on blindly with bruised, beaten, bossy, bright and shining hands.

Gillian beckons to her brother who won't look at her.

She lunges, dragging him to stand next to her. "Morgan Turner, this is Paulie—Paul, my youngest brother. I try not to come down 97 Street without him."

Morgan tilts her head, glances at Paul. There is no chance of him looking up from a table full of bitter melon to look directly at her. He is restacking the produce, trying to find a better way for the warty rinds to fit together on the slope of the tabletop display. The prosecutor has a sister and a brother. There he is, the prosecutor, barely visible in the pale shaggy face of the man in front of Morgan now.

Together, the three of them search the produce department for pomelos one more time. Gillian asks a clerk for help. No pomelos today—they have just gone out of season and supply is momentarily stalled. Morgan settles for tangerines as a hostess gift for Lilian.

"You are too legit, doing your festivals right with real Chinese people running them and everything," Gillian says. "All we have is Josh. How jealous are we? Right Paulie?"

When she finds out Morgan has come to the store on the bus, Gillian refuses to let her ride it back up the street, insists on driving her home. They have paid for their groceries and are about to leave when Gillian halts just inside the doors with a rustle of plastic bags. "*Jiaozi!*" she says, meaning to say "dumpling" but pronouncing the word more like she's saying something about a favourite son. "I forgot to get *jiaozi*. It's the only real Chinese food the kids will eat and that fitness nut mother of theirs never cooks enough." She looks all around herself, up at Paul.

"Sorry guys, I need to go back. Hey, can you two sit here?" She nods to a café table near the sliding doors, in sight of the guardian lions. She piles the grocery bags at Paul's feet, before leaving them, walking backward toward the store's freezer section. "Sorry! *Deng yi xia!*"

Grounded by the heap of groceries, Paul sits. Morgan takes the second chair at the table, pinches her hands between her knees.

Paul palms the knot of hair tied at the nape of his neck, looking out the window at the hard grey mane of the male lion. "Gillian always forgets something. Always, every time, everywhere."

Morgan nods.

Paul says, "Yeah, she's always got too much going on. And it looks like she's trying to add you to the mix. But I get it. Not everyone has a chance to fawn all over the girl whose sister got killed by some crazy guy. Yeah, that's right. We all know who you are. Gillian introduced you as Something-something Turner, right? And Josh has been obsessed with the Turner lady's case for—what is it now—a couple years already? Yeah, we all know you."

His speech is picking up speed as he goes, one foot bouncing beneath the table, jostling the grocery bags. "So don't get confused," he goes on. "Don't forget you're the one doing Gillian an honour by letting her be nice to you."

He has disturbed one of the grocery bags enough to send its open end slumping toward the floor, its cans and bottles rolling onto the tiles. He gasps but doesn't reach for them as they move away from his feet. He is still talking to Morgan even as she bends her head below the tabletop to repack the spilled bag.

"I've got to know something—from you, from your perspective as the Family of the Victim. You really think that murderer guy isn colleauges't crazy? I mean, that's the whole point of the trial, right—not that he did it but what was going through his head when he did it? That's what Josh is fighting about, right?"

Morgan lifts the bag of groceries into her lap.

Paul's fingers are in his own hair, pressed against his scalp. "So seriously, you're with Josh on this? You really believe that guy isn't crazy? I mean, for me it was one look at his mugshot on TV and I was like, 'Oh yeah. Psychotic.'"

Morgan frowns into the groceries. Coleen has explained all of this to them. In some situations, some mental illnesses are taken into account by the law and others are not. The legal test for Not Criminally Responsible is more complicated than simply flashing a prescription for psycho-active medications and—but she can't begin to say all of this to Paul Lund.

He is talking again, drumming his fingertips against his forehead now. "Because some people really are crazy. It happens all the time. Me, I'm crazy. But Josh—I'm not sure Josh believes anyone is crazy enough to be allowed to get away with anything. My brother—he's the complete opposite of crazy, which is its own kind of totally insane. All three of us are crazy in our own way. I mean—look at Gillian." He glances at Morgan. "And you—how could you not be crazy after what happened to your family?"

He uses the word "crazy" freely, easily enough to make Morgan flinch. It is a term she has never heard anyone at the courthouse use to describe mental health patients. It has got to be offensive, or something. But who is she to say that to Paul Lund? His hair is long, his complexion is deathly white from sleeping through most of his days, but he doesn't make her feel like Finnemore or like the yelling doomsayer on the bus make her feel.

From his coat pocket, Paul extracts a plastic cylinder rattling with tablets. He's saying, "Lucky for me, at least I've got pills I can take. Great pills. Best. You take pills?"

She has never taken anything but Tylenol and antibiotics.

"Nice. Me—I'm a monster without my meds. I'm getting a criminal record, you know." He turns to face her for the first time, looking for shock and fear.

Morgan is still staring into Gillian's grocery bag. Psychosis and criminal records—none of it means Paul Lund has ever hurt someone.

He tugs at his elastic and shakes his hair free. "I've never hurt anyone yet, but maybe someday. Anything can happen. You never know what's going to happen."

Gillian has queued at the cash register again. She waves a bag of frozen dumplings at them. Morgan lifts a hand to wave back.

Paul doesn't move. He keeps talking. "You know, some days, I could shave, put on a suit, and go be Josh. I could, I could do it. Other days, my life is a nightmare. What gets me most about being psychotic aren't fake voices in my head but the feeling that all the real voices around me are talking about me." He nods at the row of cash registers staffed with bored black-haired women. "If I was off my meds, I'd be convinced I accidentally dishonoured those cute clerk-ladies over there with something I said, or didn't say to them—like they're princesses in a Kung Fu movie or whatever, and once it gets dark, they'll assume their true forms as lady-knights errant and beat the sh-crap out of me, or worse." Paul grins at Morgan. "I shouldn't have said it out loud. That delusion—it's starting to grow on me already. Look at them—just look at those Kung Fu movie princesses, all lined up there, getting dragged into making small talk with Gillian and everything."

Morgan laughs, quietly but genuinely.

"Look at you," Paul chides her. "Hey, paranoia's not funny."

She apologizes but laughs again.

He is smiling too, even as he leans over the table, lowers his voice. "You can laugh, Turner, because something awful already happened to you. You already know what your monster looks like. You know what people are whispering to each other when they realize who you are. But for me, it's like something terrible is almost happening, all the time, to me, and I can't quite make out what it is."

It's wrong—it's all ignorant, mannish, ridiculous. Morgan doesn't know how to tell him, doesn't have a chance to tell him before he snaps his hair elastic against his knuckle and says, "Then there's my voice. Sometimes I take what I just said out loud and repeat it to myself, quietly, so I can hear how it sounds from far away, like I'm me and someone else at the same time, hearing what I sound like to other people."

"That's called empathy," Gillian says, arriving beside them with a bag and a receipt. "And it's perfectly normal—healthy, *necessary*. Paulie just experiences it differently than other people."

He clucks his tongue, nods at Morgan, gestures with his chin toward his sister. "Like I was telling you, Turner, she's just like him. What a pair—Gill and Josh. You see it?"

Gillian punches at his shoulder, "What are you saying to Morgan over here? Put your pills away, you weirdo. I told you, no crazy-talk at first sight."

He gets to his feet, gathers all of the bags including the one from Morgan's lap, and carries everything past the guardian lions, out into the street.

They are in Gillian's car, halfway to Sheila's house, bringing Morgan home, when Gillian asks her for a second act of friendship. "Hey, hand your phone up to Paulie so he can put my number in it."

Morgan sets her phone where he can reach it, on the console between the front seats.

Sheila's house is empty when Morgan steps inside. She goes to the TV credenza at the window, sits, but doesn't look out through the glass. Instead, she looks at her phone, at Gillian Lund's number newly keyed into the contacts list. Paul has entered it as "Sister Lund." On a contact list as short as Morgan's, she can't help but notice a second new number. It is entered as "Psycho Paul."

The morning of Lilian's festival, Morgan rides the bus for almost an hour to meet her and the rest of the Freibergs kitchen ladies at the train station. Their husbands, children, a few elderly mothers and fathers have come along. It is a massive family gathering—something Morgan hadn't foreseen. It is heavy—she is heavy—a burden and an intrusion, someone who will need everything explained and oriented, translated. Lilian sees Morgan recoiling, has expected it all along, kept the scope of the spring outing uncommunicated on purpose, accustomed now to the subtleties needed to maintain this delicate friendship. Morgan's presence here today is a burden Lilian and the others have already weighed and accepted.

She advances into Morgan's retreat, grinning, snatching the bag of tangerines from Morgan's hands, storming into a reenactment of a scene from the Korean television drama all of them have agreed is the best one ever made, one they have watched twice through—and the best episodes more times than that. Lilian flicks the train of a long silk skirt she is not actually wearing, cups one hand over the back of her neck, and recites evil mother-in-law dialogue in misspoken Korean.

Omo...dorowa!

Morgan isn't the imposter at the festival anymore but the image of everyone's favourite downtrodden Korean pop culture heroine caught in the tangerine spoiling scene from episode eleven of *Secret Garden*. The joke is universal, Lilian's best Korean is hysterically bad, the bag of tangerines is nearly spilt, and the ladies, husbands, mother, fathers, Morgan—all of them are laughing.

Shouting, her hands on each of Morgan's shoulders, pushing her from behind, Lilian steers Morgan into her minivan. Her husband calls out a welcome. His name is 黄成佑 but he tells Morgan to call him Chad as he waves her toward the back of the van. Stooped and stumbling, she finds a seat behind the elders, next to Lilian's youngest son, Howie—a beautiful, long-legged five-year-old who presents for her the entirety of human knowledge pertaining to lemurs. He is Canadian born, with fluent English, barely accented. He uses it to warn her not to assume too much about lemurs based on what they may seem to share with monkeys or with raccoons. Lemurs are just themselves.

Lilian loses track of Howie's chatter when Chad tunes the radio to the world music station and cranks the volume high. On the airwaves, a man's voice is singing a sweet love song that has been remixed to add techno-pop highlights to its guzheng strings. It's a favourite song of Chad's and he is poking Lilian in the arm at every chorus, cajoling her to join him in singing "你是我的最爱无人能代替." You are my irreplaceable beloved. She scoffs and swats his hand away—which for him, is nearly as satisfactory as her singing would be.

The convoy of vehicles moves through the innards of the city until it reaches the point where the north end of town is bisected by heavy railway lines. Just before the tracks, Chad turns a corner, into a park—dry lawns and tall trees, the city's oldest public cemetery. They roll to a stop in the corner of the graveyard where the western sides of the stones are carved with large single Chinese characters, family names. Howie is out of his restraints, pushing past Morgan's knees and the elders seated in front of them, tumbling out onto the warming, still partly frozen grass.

The adults are slower, encumbered by rakes and rags, weeding forks and wire brushes. This is what Gillian Lund knew but did not tell Morgan, what Howie knew and assumed everyone knew. Today's festival is to celebrate the progression of spring and it is also for the dead. With the rest of the party, Lilian moves through the cemetery squatting in front of headstones, wiping away dust from the highway and train yard, the droppings of the graveyard magpies who live in the pines and spruces all winter long. The families dig weeds and comb the thatch from the dormant grass. Howie is given a garbage bag and sent running from grave to grave, collecting remains of old flowers and the stubs of burnt incense. He needs to be reminded, over and over, not to disturb any fresh flowers newly left on the tops of monuments. But he is hardly listening, making noise of his own, calling "黄!" back to his father whenever he sees the word etched into a gravestone. It is their family name, and the only character Howie knows how to read.

Most of the rituals and tomb-sweeping were done last weekend, while the Freibergs ladies were at work. Today's date is less auspicious but better than nothing— better than letting all of this dry up and drift away. The tombs of the ladies' own ancestors are in another country, unreachable but not unremembered. Lilian and the others are here to serve dead strangers, graves left uncleaned, without offerings, ancestors of people like themselves who have gone too far away to care for their own.

Howie is now setting new sticks of incense in the holes bored into the bases of the stones. It will be lit and burnt, left along with single red apples set on the tops of the gravestones. The bag of apples bangs against Howie's bony knee cap as he labours from grave to grave, bruising the fruit. Morgan takes it from him. She will act as his porter, not knowing, otherwise, how to act at all. Lilian sees Morgan standing on her feet as if she's minding Howie while the rest of them are on the ground, soil beneath their fingernails. She stands herself. "Okay?" Lilian calls.

Morgan won't interrupt Howie's talk and answers with a sign, circling her fingers to show she's OK.

The tomb-sweeping work is light and finished quickly. When it's done, they move to a nearby park without any graves in it. It is not a special place, just an open space. Canada's greatest resource is emptiness. In the wide field, the ladies unfold flimsy aluminum tables and everyone sits to eat. In the near distance, Chad is helping Howie fly a kite. High wind can be counted on in springtime and the kite rises easily into the sky. It was made in China, not as an heirloom but as merchandise for the dollar store where Lilian bought handfuls of them for the picnic. The sail of Howie's kite is plastic and decorated with a bootlegged cartoon character. Its features dim as he uncoils the string, the kite curving upward into a blue sky.

It flies high enough for its colour to become indistinguishable. At its highest, it looks as small and dark as the back of Howie's head.

Chad looks away from the boy, over his shoulder, toward the women. They lean into each other, speaking with low voices, as if Chinese doesn't do enough to obscure their talk. Lilian waves at Chad across the field—sharply, a different kind of swat than the one from the front seat of the minivan. He takes the skein of kite string from Howie and presses something into his hand. The boy waves the object over his head, jumps and twirls once in a circle before his father lays a hand on his arm to calm him down, pointing at the line strung taut in front of them. Howie extends his hand.

The boy has cut the kite string. No one told Morgan it would happen and she gasps. Free from the spool, the kite and its line fly away as everyone cheers. Howie runs after it, waving his arms as if to propel it along. The elders are calling to him to drop the scissors if he wants to run. There is no need to translate it.

Lilian spills a shopping bag of cheap kites onto the tabletop for anyone who wants one. Howie comes capering, looking for a second, a kite that will not be cut away. Lilian unwraps one and hands it to Morgan. Morgan pauses, waiting for a clue to tell her whether declining a kite would be the rejection of a cherished tradition, or just the everyday rudeness of refusing a friend's kind offer. Lilian knows neither is possible for Morgan. She nods as Morgan takes the kite. The cartoon character on its sail is a toy train with a face—bulging eyes and hard, domed grey cheeks. Prodded by his mother, one of the older boys helps Morgan launch it. It rises into the sky, wind pulling hard at the sail, uncoiling the spool of string almost against Morgan's will. Throughout the field, Howie's scissors are being handed from one flyer to another. Some people use them, others simply pass them on. Kites are cut loose and carried away, over the highway and the train yard, beyond all reach—blowing eastward, the long way home.

Lilian is by Morgan's side again. "很好, 很好," she says, because, as Morgan now knows, it means approval, and Morgan's kite is flying well. In one hand, Lilian holds the scissors, and in the other she holds onto Howie's arm.

"Your turn to cut it," he tells her.

Morgan looks to Lilian, still unsure what any of this means.

Lilian shrugs. "Do it or don't, either is fine." She is not merely holding onto Howie, she is holding him back. She is alternating between smiling at Morgan, offering her the scissors, and tugging at a squirming Howie, reprimanding him.

Morgan steps toward the boy. Offering her kite string. Howie can cut it. It doesn't matter.

"No, no, no," Lilian says. "It definitely matters."

Morgan takes the scissors from her, seeing it's the best way to get Howie to stop struggling against his mother. When they see she has taken them, the rest of the kitchen ladies—Melanie, Anita, Phoenix—they gather, quiet and waiting. Phoenix presses her palms together, points her fingers upward, as if she is about to pray.

In their stillness, the wind presses harder against Morgan's face, her open eyes. She blinks, and Lilian sees she and her colleagues are exposed. Morgan sees now what they have never shown her—what has never been spoken of in her presence, not in a way she could understand. They know. All of Morgan's friends from the factory know who Tricia was and what she should have meant to Morgan. As they stand together on the brown spring grass where she anchors her kite, Morgan knows Lilian and the ladies have read the articles, seen the photos, the footage of the tarp in the field, Sheila on the courthouse steps, Marc in his headset microphone, Finnemore's madman mugshot, his dating website profile picture—everything. They have known, maybe since the very beginning. This outing, this tomb-sweeping festival and the flying of kites—they may be meant for the ladies' faraway dead, for the lonesome dead in the Edmonton cemetery, but they are also meant for Tricia.

Morgan is taking too long. Howie is in agony. "Cut it," he says. And then he's clapping his hands, chanting, "Cut it, cut it."

Morgan holds the scissors, all the wrong fingers in all the wrong holes. Lilian nudges her with one shoulder. Morgan opens the blades, fits them around the thin line of nylon connecting her to the kite.

Maybe it was the wind. No one watching could say. The kite on the end of Morgan's line surges eastward, the spool slips from her grip, and the kite flies away on its own—no cutting, no cheering. Howie takes one quick step forward to chase the spool as it bounces along the grass before Lilian hauls him back. At the far end of the field, the kite is moving over the fence dividing the park from the highway, sinking, its string falling over the pavement, draping itself in a loose swag across the narrow upper edge of the high chain link fence of the train yard, the sail somewhere beyond, not quite vanished.

By nightfall, Morgan is home, still too full from the picnic to eat dinner. Maybe she will crash through the apple Howie pressed on her as she was leaving him in the backseat of the van—the prettiest of all the apples he had been told to leave behind as an offering in the cold graveyard, the one he had kept anyway. He was never hungry for it—it's just fruit—but he rescued it anyway, turned it into a blessing for someone still alive.

She sets it on a shelf in the refrigerator, outside the crisper where the apple's perfect Red Delicious skin, buffed shiny by Howie's grubby hands, wouldn't be polluted by the runny juices of a spoiling cucumber the whole family has been pretending not to notice. She closes the refrigerator door, but a yellow light remains in the dark house. Its source is somewhere in the basement, casting a small patch of light on the wall by the backdoor. In the daylight, someone must have missed it before leaving this morning, left it burning all day.

Morgan won't cut the kite string, won't eat the apple, but she will find the light and turn it out. Its colour signals warmth, and after spending a day entirely outside for the first time in years, Morgan is cold. She stops to sit in the beam of light on the basement steps, each of her palms pressed to the tread of the stair beneath her. When she moves her head, she can smell the traces of graveyard incense still in her hair. Edmonton is a large city with many cemeteries. Tricia is buried in one much bigger than the one Morgan visited today. It is on the far northern edge of the city—a sprawling field along a utility corridor. If Tricia's cemetery has a Chinese section, fragrant with smoking incense, Morgan has never seen it. She has been to that graveyard only once, when Sheila sent her and Tod to see the newly installed headstone. They hadn't left anything behind, no offering. They had burned nothing, but Tod had kicked at a dandelion growing out of the turf, twisted his toe against its yellow head like the butt of a cigarette.

Tricia's body is buried away from home but the rest of her is here, beneath the stairs where Morgan now sits, in the lowest, darkest place in the house. The space under the stairs has a lightbulb with a pull-string switch, short rolls of surplus linoleum from when Sheila had the kitchen floor redone, and dozens of torn black garbage bags overflowing with clothing. It is the room where everything Tricia owned is stored, unsorted but saved.

Tricia must have died sometime close to the tomb-sweeping festival of 2014. Her funeral came months later, after her remains were found, the police press conference and forensics were finished, and Finnemore's prosecution was beginning to form. Sheila and Marc went together to the funeral home to make arrangements, their grim good will for each other eroding with every detail to be decided—the flowers and menus and politics of the grand tragic public drama of Tricia's funeral. They would stage the perfect tribute, though Tricia would know nothing of it—like an elaborate first birthday party for a baby.

Two days before the funeral, Morgan had gone with her mother under the basement stairs. Tricia's apartment had been cleared soon after she stopped being a missing person. Hardly any place stays a dedicated crime scene for long. The police released the apartment and the landlord had all of Tricia's things stuffed into trash bags that Sheila and Tod carted away eight at a time—as many as would fit into either of their small cars—until they were all moved here.

No one disturbed Tricia's belongings until the funeral director asked the family to bring something nice for Tricia to wear inside her casket. She had amassed an immense supply of clothes. If anything was her life's work, it might be this.

"It's a sham," Sheila said, tugging at the pull switch and ducking underneath the stairs. "How can they talk about dressing what's left of her? It can't be done. This is a farce meant to make what's happened seem less grotesque."

Morgan knew it. She had read about it, late at night, alone in her room, on her computer screen. Remains like Tricia's would be put inside a bag, in pieces—usually a soft white drawstring bag, not unlike the ones upscale stores use to wrap expensive new purses, to protect the leather finish and make them seem worth the prices paid for them. Being dressed in a bag was not normal, and part of a funeral seemed to be to make everything look like nothing much had changed. But changing into being dead should be normal. That's what Morgan thought. What is more normal than a change that happens to everyone, like dying? It wasn't that dying wasn't normal, it was that trying to force death to walk parallel to life still going on around it, to mime and mimic it—dead Tricia wearing the clothes she bought at the mall, dropped on the floor—this is what was not normal. It felt wrong. It felt like this.

"I'll tell you what we'll do, Morgan. We will find the skimpiest, sluttiest dress in here and bring them that—answer their sham with one of our own. What'll they say to that?" Sheila was deep under the stairs, tossing out the lightest bags, the ones she could tell were full of clothing rather than Tricia's books or dishes.

"You think they'll want shoes too? A nice pair of platform stilettos—something sparkly?" A heap of clothing and torn garbage bags filled the space at the bottom of the stairs, covering Morgan's feet. "Why wasn't this one of the options on the schedule of services at the funeral home? Maybe we should start a family business, hey Morgan? A business putting together smashing outfits for dead girls. Nice family business. We'll give it your father's name."

A shoe came hurtling out from under the stairs, not a stiletto but a pink foam clog, bundled up and carelessly preserved by the apartment building manager, worth no more nor less to him than anything else Tricia owned.

Sheila stepped out of the doorway of the storage space, stooped as if she'd hit herself on the stairs overhead too many times to risk standing upright anymore. "This is the last bag with clothes in it. It's got to be the fancy dresses."

Sheila tore into the plastic with her fingernails. It was not a block of miscellaneous clothing that came tumbling from inside but a single garment, maybe a blanket—a silky white blanket embellished with beads and lace.

No, that wasn't right. Sheila crushed a handful of tulle crinoline against her palm. This was a wedding dress— not a gag one salvaged from a divorced girl-friend or the costume rack at a thrift shop. It was a brand-new winter-white mermaid-style wedding dress with the tags and fraud prevention cords still attached.

"This—this is the one. Pack it up, Morgan. This is the one for the funeral home, this is the one for the coffin." Sheila threw the dress at Morgan's head. Layers of skirts blocked her sight but she could still hear Sheila laughing. Sheila was bending to sit on the pile of Tricia's clothes, tossing black bras stained white at the armholes into the air, her laughter tightening into short heaving breaths. "Take it away," she said, waving Morgan up the stairs, as-sembling a private space, an empty, uninhabited place to receive her grief. "For god's sake, Morgan. Take it."

Morgan had obeyed, carried Tricia's new-with-tags wedding dress up the stairs, away from their mother. She threaded its skirts through a hanger, folding them into a garment bag. Tricia was buried in the same casket as the white dress. As far as Morgan knows, nobody at the funeral lifted the lid, no one knows the dress is in there with the bag of bones but Sheila, the funeral director, and Morgan herself. Did the funeral people ever snip the price tags off?

At least it was white, Morgan tells herself now, on the evening of her first tomb-sweeping festival. It was white like the clothing of an old-fashioned ghost on Korean television, always dressed in long-sleeved white robes. These were normal grave clothes--nothing to sort or select, nothing to protest or pretend, nothing to fake or make a mockery of, nothing but everyone made the same, if only at the very end.

10

Father's Day—the celebration of the celebrated, the nois-
ing of the noisy, the fourth of July of the family holi-
days—is a picnic for Marc Turner. He doesn't always see
his children on Father's Day. It's more of a biennial event
for the Turners, and this is their year. He will visit with
his children but not at his home—an extremely rustic
cottage in the woods west of the city, on a lake, with a
woman who is nothing like a mother to either of Marc's
kids. Since his divorce from Sheila, Marc has wanted his
children's attention but not their scrutiny, esteem without intimacy—to be more like their father-in-law than
like their father.

In another unnamed city park—an empty green space
with one wooden picnic table defaced with love letters
and slander in the middle of the suburbs, within sight of
Sheila's house—he gathers his living children. Marc's girlfriend, Julie, brings most of the food for the Father's Day
picnic. This year's entrée is imported American corn on the
cob, too cold by the time it's served for butter to melt on
it. Morgan is rummaging through shopping bags, looking
for paper plates while Julie apologizes and Marc shouts

her down with jolly bawling. "It's a picnic, Jules. Everyone's free from the tyranny of dinnerware at a picnic."

Al fresco is the order of the day simply because Sheila doesn't like Marc, not because she's trying to encourage their kids to remain distant from him. In fact, she has been telling them to spend more time with him ever since he called her, threatening to "reopen the divorce" and get a court to force her to let them see him.

"They're grown adults, Marc. Leave the court, leave me, leave everyone but the kids' own guilty consciences out of it."

Marc sits on the picnic table's bench, beside Tod, who is pulling stray strands of corn silk out of the cob he is about to eat. The hands that shucked them were not as thorough as the scalder. He is flicking a yellow-green thread from the ends of his fingers, into the grass as Marc slaps his back, laughing. "Eat up, son, before you waste away."

Tod doesn't even sigh.

Julie sits down on the bench. "Stop it, Marc."

"Remember, Morgie, when your brother was little—a little angel-faced, dark-haired boy?"

She doesn't remember. Tricia, Tod's older sister, might have some memory of him as a small child. Morgan is younger and in her mind, Tod has never been smaller than the size and close to the weight of a torpedo. This is how she knows him, this is how she likes him. Anyway, Tod doesn't like angels, says they're as fake and stupid as unicorns and fairies—though why unicorns and fairies should bother anyone is beyond Morgan.

"My boy has a man's face now," Marc says. He rubs his own jaw with his hand, like an actor on a stage, playing at thoughtfulness. "Hey, you know who you've grown up to remind me of, Tod?"

Tod raises a cold, hairy cob of corn to his mouth, shielding his face.

"Look at him, Julie," Marc says. "November 22, 1963—a day history was made on live TV. You must have been watching that day, weren't you, Jules?"

She snorts. "How should I know? I would've been a baby in 1963."

Marc laughs. "Sure, maybe. But you've been alive long enough to have seen the newsreel footage a hundred times over by now. Look at my boy there, and imagine him with an old black bowler hat on his head instead of that ball cap."

Julie squints at Tod across the picnic table. "Okay."

"And now," Marc says, "think November 1963."

She shakes her head. "I got nothing, Marc. It's not a Kennedy thing again, is it?"

"Precisely."

"Here we go with the Kennedys…"

"Come on," he insists. "It was in Texas, during a jail transfer of the suspected shooter right after John F. Kennedy was killed. The whole thing was broadcast straight to my living room. Big man in a suit and hat comes running out of the crowd, and the announcer starts yelling, 'He's been shot, he's been shot. Lee Harvey Oswald has been shot.' It was like a gangster movie only with the gunshot sound effects all dull and slow."

Julie is frowning. "Your boy looks like Oswald?"

"No, the other man on the play. Jack Ruby." Marc claps his hands one time. "Yes! You see what I mean." Marc slaps the wooden tabletop. "I can see it. I can still see it. I mean, come on, you don't forget something like sitting on the couch as a kid and seeing someone get mortally wounded on live television. Jack Ruby, sitting right here at the picnic table with me on Father's Day—just change the hat…"

Tod drops a stripped cob into a napkin. "Not gonna work. I'm not gonna spring out and shoot anyone dead on the way to the courthouse for you. Thanks for dinner, Julie. I'm heading back, Morgo."

The three of them watch Tod cross the park lawn, walking back to Sheila's house. Julie cracks a beer from her purse and pours it into a sports bottle. "Every single time…"

Marc crumples an empty shopping bag between his hands. "What do you think he weighs now? He's always been a big boy but—come on, he's got to be three hundred pounds—maybe closer to four. How'd he let himself get like that? He can get away with it at this age but once he starts to get a little older—blood pressure, blood sugar, knees, everything—it'll blow. It all comes back to what happened, doesn't it, Morgie? If he could forgive Brett, then maybe he could go back to being a regular fat guy instead of—of…" Marc waves his arm toward Tod's back moving out of sight at the edge of the park.

"It's all related. I can't forgive Brett on Tod's behalf, but I sure would if I could."

Julie hands Morgan the sports bottle. Morgan rolls it between her hands. They are not really family, not yet spit-sisters, still uninitiated when it comes to each other's saliva. Through the straw in the bottle, the beer smells warm and doughy. Morgan passes it to Marc.

He drags hard on the straw. "Honestly, you'd think working with all those dead hogs he'd be a little more self-aware—have a better idea where he's at and where it's all heading if he doesn't do something. It's working for Morgan. You're not too porky yet, are you honey?"

She crosses her arms over her middle.

"As it is," Marc goes on, "that job, his whole life-style—it's the long slow proof of his self-loathing, that death wish of his, only now, it comes with a pay cheque."

"Aw, give it a rest, Marc." Julie reaches past Morgan to take the bottle from him.

Flipping away from this tired, painful channel, Morgan asks Marc for a favour. In the course of his long, sorted career, before the family moved north, he sold cars. Thanks to the Freibergs employees' collective agreement, Morgan has been able to save $3,000, enough to free her from riding the bus as long as she can find a car that will run without any repairs for that price.

"You bet I'll find you something, Morgie. No problem." Marc rubs his hands together, playing someone who can't wait to get started. They spend the rest of the evening in Marc's car, parked on the street close enough to Sheila's house to use her Wi-Fi signal, Julie sleepy with purse-beer in the backseat, Marc and Morgan browsing local ads for cars for sale. This chase after the phantom of a perfect $3,000 car—it's the best Father's Day present Morgan has ever given him. Morgan goes inside when Sheila's Wi-Fi signal abruptly disappears precisely at 9 p.m.

"Run along, Morgie. Looks like your mother is calling you in for the night." That's what Marc said, driving away, promising to be back once he'd found some used cars for them to test drive.

Sheila's house is quiet. Light shines from the crack underneath her bedroom door but from nowhere else. Morgan steps up to Tod's closed, dark door. His shift starts at five in the morning tomorrow and he's trying to sleep. Morgan doesn't knock on the door but listens through it, tunes her hearing to the sound of fuzzy electric suction— the promise Tod will wake up in the morning.

We don't trust ourselves to resurface from sleep on our own. We stand machines beside our beds all night, contraptions meant to bring us back. When Morgan and Tricia were in school, it was a radio with fake woodgrain and the red numbers, crackling commercials into their bedroom at 7:17am. Morgan doesn't remember what Tod used to wake himself up. It must have been an alarm clock a lot like theirs. It isn't anymore. A year before Tricia died, the machine beside Tod's bed that kept him waking up every morning became medical equipment—a device that sucks air from the room and blows it up his nose, into his throat while he sleeps.

The machine came along with Tod's diagnosis of sleep apnea—a diagnosis they will never reveal to Marc. When laid out flat, Tod's body turned onto its back, everything slowly collapses under the weight of itself during the night, his throat pinching closed around his airways. Sleep apnea is like belated crib death for grownups—bed death, going gentle into that good night, snoring and choking against the dying of the light.

The machine is called a CPAP which, as everyone knows, means "continuous positive airway pressure." It's an unworkable name for everyday conversation and demands an acronym. Morgan understands that, but she knows what everyone in the doctors' office means when they say "pap," and frankly, it's embarrassing to hear her brother talking about it in terms of his face. In her mind, Tod's CPAP is called by another name, the brand-name moulded into the plastic of its base. The name is "Dreamweaver3000" which is also embarrassing, like something their white elementary school music teachers with fringe jackets might have chosen.

Dreamweaver3000 looks like a tabletop humidifier—a fancy bowl of water and a small motor that's a bit too loud. The whole thing might pass for normal if it weren't for the mask attachment. On the end of a long, clear hose is a plastic cone big enough to fit over Tod's nose. It's not a dainty cannula, like a prop from a movie where someone is beautifully, poignantly sick. Tod's sleep apnea is a real medical issue—an ugly, bulky situation—and Dreamweaver3000 is the beginnings of a scaled down respirator.

The mask is meant to be lashed to Tod's head, tied to his cranium by three straps, one running right between his eyes, over the top of his head.

When the machine was new, he tried it on for Morgan, proving it was no big deal. "Just like that, Morgo." He cranked the buckle of the strap under his ear, tightening the mask until the flesh of his nearly-bald scalp puckered around the straps. As a nurse, Sheila says the odds of Tod's snoring escalating to dying in his sleep are slim, but the constant wear of all those small suffocations will grind down his heart and brain, shorten his life. Dreamweaver3000 is real medicine, covered by the Freibergs enhanced healthcare plan. It is as uncomfortable and difficult as any real medicine, and as important.

Dreamweaver3000 first appeared during Tod's aspiring telomere repairman phase—that time when he was keenly interested in human longevity. All mankind needed was for someone to figure out how to keep the end pieces of our genes from getting shorter and shorter every time our cells divide, and then death and aging would become preventable diseases. He watched people talking about it in YouTube videos, read all the related Wikipedia articles, bought a book about it and everything. It was perfect. If no one ever had to step into the void, it didn't matter whether the void was actually empty or not. If death was nothing, then death could be nothing.

Maybe it was in solidarity with Tricia that Tod stopped using Dreamweaver3000 not long after her remains were found. Tricia is part of death now. It's the only place left for him to find her. There had to be something natural, bearable, beautiful within it. Death can't be a hell of cold nothingness to be avoided at all costs, at the cost of a hose strung between the eyes every night. Tod went off immortality. The new phase was marked by the quiet of his bedroom. The water in the Dreamweaver3000 reservoir evaporated to bands of crusty white lime where the hard city tap water had been.

It was Sheila who put an end to it. She filled the reservoir, wiped the dust from the black plastic, reached behind Tod's bed, and plugged the machine back into the wall. "I don't know what you're playing at, Tod, but every night you sleep here in my house, you sleep with this god-awful thing wrapped around your head."

Marc is back in the city with a notebook full of phone numbers and addresses—the locations of cars to test-drive with Morgan. "Now listen, Morgie. Your role is to stand there and say nothing. Look mean, like you hate everything. No, sweetie, not like—you gotta be prepared to walk away. Don't go falling in love before we beat them down to our price."

It takes all day—an entire day of watching Marc look under hoods, wagging his finger at bald tires and rusted wheel wells, an entire day of hearing people tell him, "Look dude, I don't know what you expect from a $3,000 car…"

Before the bank closes in the afternoon, Marc leans on the counter, watching Morgan sign for a draft for all of her savings plus next month's bus pass budget.

They have found her a car—a little car, the much older sister of Sheila's own Hyundai. It will be good on gas and easy to park. If Morgan was silly, she would name it after one of her favourite male roles from South Korean television—not one of the main romantic leads with his volatile, punchy love. She would give her car the name of one the sweet second male leads, the punchy guy's rival who always ends up alone bleeding from his lip. She would call it Kang Shinwoo, after one of her best-loved but unfavoured sides of a television love triangle—the nice guy she would have chosen if she had been the female lead posing as a boy in a K-pop idol band, taking the place of that stupid heroine who fell for the bad boy.

"Wrong one, wrong one." Lilian and the ladies had laughed at her when she stood up, turned her back, and went to clean out the dishwasher filters rather than sit and watch the final episode of poor Kang Shinwoo's series— the one where his heart breaks. "Second lead syndrome," Lilian laughed. "You got it bad."

11

Alone in the poorly lit alleyway behind Sheila's house, locked inside her new car, Morgan writes and rewrites the text message—the one with her own name in it, and the Golden Grocery store's, and the line about how she is sure she has already been forgotten. Her phone slots the recipient's name into the proper field as soon as Morgan types the first letter of "Psycho Paul."

Send.

He will find the message in the morning, when he wakes up to—do whatever he does all day. Morgan has deliberately waited until now to send it, engineering a delay meant to give her time to reassemble the strength she expended writing and sending this message—the first message she has ever sent to a man outside her family without an extremely functional purpose.

Morgan unclasps her seat belt, fails to pull her keys out of her car's ignition, triggering the high, round-edged tone of an alarm. She apologizes to Kang Shinwoo. Yes, when no one is around—and no one ever is—the car can be spoken to, addressed by the name it has succeeded in taking after all, a name Morgan never says out loud.

Its alarm ends and the car is quiet—small and plastic but not uncomfortable. If something happened, and Sheila and the house were gone, Morgan might be able to sleep in her car. It couldn't be much more difficult for her than sleeping in a bed has been lately. Maybe it's the season, all the summer sunlight keeping her awake. Or maybe it's the approach of the Finnemore trial. The summer that is beginning now will last only eight weeks at this latitude. When it ends, when the nights go dark again, the trial will begin. There is much to be done before then.

Morgan's phone buzzes against her fingers with a new message.

"Sure. Tangerines when there were no pomelos."

There he is—Psycho Paul Lund. There is no delay, no time for Morgan to think of anything but a defence. She types. Reminding him he left his number in her phone.

"I did."

He is either coy or stupid. She doesn't like either. She had meant to ask him a favour for tomorrow night. But he is here in her phone now, too soon.

It is one o'clock in the morning but he writes, "I just got up," and then, "Where are you?"

This is happening, somehow—a midnight social visit with a mentally ill man Morgan hardly knows. How did it happen for Tricia? No, this is different from Tricia's story. Tricia did know Finnemore—knew him intimately, for over a year. Coleen the paralegal says love makes it more likely, not less likely that people will hurt each other, make criminals of themselves. Tonight's story is not like that.

134

Morgan is looking for someone to come with her to see something she has been wanting to witness for herself—something sad and scary enough for her to not want to go alone. Tod and Sheila are both working night shifts this week, and neither of them would have agreed to come with her anyway. She has not asked. She won't. Morgan currently has only two people in her life whom she has heard refer to her as a friend. At this hour—at nearly every hour outside work—Lilian will be consumed with Howie and his brother, even if it's just sleeping so she can wake up and care for them in the morning. She is difficult to contact by text anyway. Most of their exchanges are variations on intricate emojis drawn with punctuation marks.

The other person to call her a friend is Gillian. If Morgan knew her better, if they were the friends Gillian wants them to be, she would know Gillian stays up late every night with her trial transcripts, reading and writing. But Morgan knows none of this, and she continues to leave Gillian unburdened, alone.

There is one contact left in Morgan's phone—one not-unfriendly contact with nowhere to go and nothing expected of him in the morning. Paul Lund does indeed look like he just got out of bed when Morgan arrives at his apartment building. His clothes have the soft, wrinkled look of the wardrobe of a person who doesn't own a washing machine and can't seem to organise the stacks of coins he would need to do laundry very often. For a moment, the orange floodlights over the doorstep of his building give his skin a glowing ruddiness it does not actually have. Morgan sees it from her car, where she waits, no thought of being asked inside the building.

He opens the door, bends to sit in the passenger seat. Paul's hair is not tied up tonight but held against his head beneath a knitted hat too loosely woven to be a winter toque.

"Turner—Hello."

She steers away from the curb slowly, signaling into the empty street.

"Nice. You're a good driver—careful, I mean. No one can ever take careful away from us."

Never more than on summer nights is downtown a terrible mess of construction—cranes, flashing amber lights, closed roads. Morgan leaves it, crossing a ravine into the west side of the city. The streets widen, darken. Paul doesn't ask where they are going. What he asks is, "What do you have for music in here?"

Morgan doesn't "have" music. She hears it on radios, in stores, in the restaurants where she has worked, in other people's spaces. For Morgan, music is not something to have, it is something to be borne.

"Nothing? Wish I'd known," Paul says. "I would have grabbed some CDs. What kind of stuff do you like, anyways?"

Both hands on the wheel, she shrugs one shoulder—the universal sign for "whatever."

Paul clicks his tongue. "That's no good. We'll work on that."

They drive to where there are no more houses, no stores, no other cars on the roads. Paul scrolls through every radio frequency, point by point, until he finds a song from the video game soundtrack he knows looping and looping on the university's student station at the bottom of the dial. There are no lyrics, but he hums the melody, undeterred by its high electronic voice. Morgan steers the car into a large parking lot outside what looks like an enormous white shipping crate—towering walls clad in aluminum, four perfect corners on its flat roof, no windows above the main floor. They have come to Freibergs.

"Like, Freibergs all-beef hot dogs?"

Not all of them are all-beef. This is the hog operation, where she works in the cafeteria during the day.

"Sweet. That's how you can afford this car." Paul pats Kang Shinwoo's dashboard as if he understands its secret personification. "I gave up my car when I went on the big meds. It said to, right on the pill bottle. I get too groggy to drive. And I'm broke anyways."

Morgan leans into the steering wheel, looking toward the roof where the "Come Join Us" billboard stands in the dark. She has never been to the factory so late. The kitchen isn't staffed at night. But Tod is supposed to be here right now, on hair removal and sanitation—the scalder.

Paul nods. "Cool. Hardcore."

She sighs because it isn't. By the time they reach sanitation and hair removal, the hogs are already dead—nothing but meat.

Paul drops his hands from the dash. "Hey, we're not

here for, like, animal liberation purposes or anything, right?"

Not at all. What Morgan wants is to see a living hog walk into Freibergs on its own four feet, like everyone here says they do. They say the hogs just stroll into the abattoir, like nosy dogs, trying to smell everything, not even scared. She can imagine it, but feels a need to witness it.

Paul looks through the windshield into the sky, to the northern horizon where a distant golden light moves over the purple edge of the world all night, every summer night. He says, "As a lamb to the slaughter...so he openeth not his mouth." He knows to apologize. "Sorry, that's not me. That's the Bible. You want someone to start quoting sad, intense, grisly stuff to you, bring a kid raised on scriptures to a slaughterhouse. You know the Bible?"

All she knows is the Christmas stuff.

"You know it better than you think. Everyone does. What people don't always know is that the Bible is full of dead and dying animals—cut them like this, burn them up like this, it'll remind you how hard it is to be God."

She turns away from her window, toward him.

He is flattening his hat against the sides of his head, tucking his hair behind his ears. "Don't trust me on any of this. I'm not churchy anymore. But Josh is. Gillian too— you must've noticed."

She hadn't. People who have never been religious themselves do not always know it when they see religion in other people. It is all around, familiar, mundane enough that people who don't live by faith think they must understand what it's like, what they think it ought to look like on someone else. Scripture is everywhere, arising like this sometimes—unannounced, unexplained in an awkwardly worded phrase, an obscure metaphor, an overstatement like the one Paul has just made. When it happens, it's like running a boat aground, finding out the substance below the surface runs higher than expected. It leaves the non-religious stranded on land that feels like a sandbar to them but may be the edge of a continental shelf for someone else.

Paul Lund doesn't excuse himself, doesn't apologize, doesn't recite a sophisticated treatise, or try to shove anyone else's head underwater as he explains why he doesn't practice his religion anymore. "I don't want to do it. Church life is hard. It's like the whole missionary thing—it doesn't end when you get home from Taiwan or Montreal or Arkansas or wherever. It does not end, just goes on and on until the end of the world, and then some. Our church is worse than most for that. Everyone there is a minister, with stuff to do and people to see. Never let anyone tell you religion is an easy way out of a hard reality. It's not easy, and all of its ways lead in, not out."

Her seat creaks beneath her. He was a missionary? In Montreal?

He smirks. "No, Gillian was in Montreal. She was the magnificent *Soeur Lund*. Josh was Taiwan. I have no idea what they called him there. I was the one in Arkansas. Elder Lund, nineteen years old. It was easier to get approved to be a missionary back then. They'd never let me go now. I wore the uniform, tried not to work too hard in the heat, kept my family happy for two years. Everyone down there always asked if I was mad I didn't get sent somewhere foreign, and I was like, 'Dude, I'm from Canada. This is foreign.'"

A racket sounds outside, across the asphalt—something loud enough for them to hear it through the glass of the car's windows. Two massive bay doors in the side of Freibergs's outer shell have opened like a pair of giant, sleepy, glowing eyes, ready to receive the long, dirty livestock liners which are coming to bring hogs to the factory.

Morgan steps out into the parking lot.

Paul opens his door, sets one foot on the ground and gags at the barnyard smell diffusing from the open bay doors. He is ranting, swearing behind his hand cupped over his mouth and nose, but he's following Morgan anyway. They move toward the loading bay, closer to the electric light from inside the factory. There is a strip of grass between two concrete curbs at the edge of the Freibergs lot. Morgan sits in the grass, and when Paul doesn't, she pulls at the sleeve of his jacket. The stench is like smoke when a house is on fire. Get low to stay out of it. He sits, uncovers his face.

The animals come as early in the morning as anyone can stand to bring them, especially in the summer when it can get hot. Pigs don't sweat and they heat up and die when the sun is out and there's nothing to wallow in. To see them arrive here, it's easier to stay up all night.

Morgan and Paul wait, the light in the sky growing. The colours in Paul's toque begin to reveal themselves—blue, red, and orange. He shifts sideways, grazing Morgan's arm with his.

She wants to know something badly enough not to recoil. She will stay close and she will ask him if there are pigs in the Bible.

Paul rubs his eyes, sniff the cuffs of his sleeves before dropping his hands from his face. "Yeah, there's a whole bunch of them. It's weird, actually. There's this story about Jesus, traveling around, like He did. And He's on this crazy island where He runs into a guy who's possessed by a bunch of demons."

Morgan's face flushes in the dark. She hadn't asked about demons.

"The demons come first," Paul explains, "then the pigs. It's okay. You need a fair bit of evil stuff kicking around or nothing else in the Bible makes much sense. Okay, so the possessed guy sees Jesus and comes running out, yelling."

Along with the Christmas story, Morgan knows something about the Easter story—the one where Jesus gets killed. Is this how it starts? Do the demons pick a fight with Him and start the crucifixion?

"What? No, what is the matter with you? It's not a video game. Jesus doesn't fight monsters and beat bosses. Demons can't kill Him. They can't kill anyone—not without a lot of human help. They're useless—incorporeal. They're all wispy and invisible. Like, they can't even

141

turn a doorknob or make a sandwich. It's embarrassing."

Paul plucks a blade of grass, splits it along its central vein with his fingernail. "So the demons are all talking to Jesus, calling Him by name and begging Him to leave them alone and let them keep living inside this poor guy. But they're the worst tenants. They've kept the guy up all night for years—naked, freaking out in graveyards, cutting himself, and so much crying. Anyways, there's no way Jesus is going to let the demons keep that up and they know it so they try negotiating. There's this big herd of pigs feeding not too far away and the demons ask if they can possess the bodies of the pigs instead of the man's." Paul stops, nodding toward Freibergs, winding the bisected blade of grass around his forefinger, silent, stuck.

Morgan waits beside him for the rest of the story— waits long enough to touch his arm again, on purpose this time. She needs to know how it ends.

"Give me a sec," he says. "I don't think I can say it. Not out loud."

It doesn't matter. Morgan needs to hear the rest. The spirit of Reverend Vreend is here with them outside the Freibergs pork packing plant—or at least the familiar spirit of the shared religious imagination that runs through Paul Lund and Len Vreend and all the rest of them. It is an imagination she has never been made a part of, but it is here now, nodding, eyes glistening in the loading bay lights. In Paul Lund, it is weak, sick and teary but it can still hear her, still sense her waiting with her questions about evil, and how to cast it out—not with fake, brutal sham exorcisms like Finnemore's lie about his attack on demons in Tricia's ear, but with true purifications. On the Bible pigs' island, in the hockey arena, anywhere at all—does it work, is it real? She nudges Paul again, prodding him toward the rest of the story of how god Himself would conduct an exorcism.

Paul's shoulders lurch forward, as if he has been clenched in a lifesaving anti-choking manoeuvre. "What? Exorcism? An exorcism—no it's not like that. Jesus doesn't have to do exorcisms. He doesn't yell and cast spells, like some terrified phony. Demons just have to leave when he says the word."

There is a word?

"He is the Word."

Jesus is the word?

Paul yells a laugh, shoves Morgan sideways. She plants one elbow into the grass to keep from falling, glances toward the loading bay doors for any sign that someone inside hears him. He's wiping his eyes. "Yes, the Word. Exactly. Now you've got it."

The religious imagination can be kind of a mess.

"Anyways, demons have to leave when He tells them to," Paul says. "Simple as that. They don't have a choice. God can always get His way—which can be awful frickin' confusing, actually."

There is still an ellipse at the end of all Paul has said. There is more. Morgan should let it go, like she always does, like she wishes Howie and the cafeteria ladies had let her go when she stood in the park with the scissors and the kite string. She presses him anyway—apologizes, but has to know what happens to the pigs.

He swallows, takes a breath. "When the demons are sent out of the man, he's okay—normal again. But no one is thankful. Everyone is scared, trying to get Jesus to leave the island without doing anything else to upset the well-adjusted demon equilibrium everyone had learned to live with. Typical, right?"

One more nudge.

"The pigs—thousands of them—they stampede off a cliff and into the sea. They drown. All together—they die." Paul shivers against Morgan's arm. His hands cover his face. He is crying just as loudly as he had been laughing moments before. He is bowing into his lap, sitting on the sod outside Freibergs flagship hog processing plant at dawn with a strange tragic woman, expounding scriptures to her, weeping into the palms of his hands.

Morgan has very little experience with adult crying. Despite Tricia's death, the Turners have not cried together as part of their mourning. All she knows of comforting others is what she remembers from when she was a child. She pats Paul's back, shushing him. The story of the demons and the pigs was supposed to have happened 2,000 years ago. Even in the happiest story ever, all those pigs would be dead by now, of natural causes.

He sobs out a laugh, wipes his eyes with his sleeve. "Natural causes—that's right," Paul stammers through what's left of his tears. "Don't—don't get the wrong idea, okay? Jesus didn't kill the pigs. Neither did the demons—

they can't. Remember? It wasn't a good versus evil thing. It's just—I guess—guess that running into the sea to stick it to demons is just—just natural—what all decent pigs would do."

Paul breathes deeply at Morgan's side. She is still patting his back, musing about the story's horrible waste of meat.

He laughs again, palms the top of her head, nods toward Freibergs. "This place messed you up. And the Bible people were mostly Jews, so meat wasn't really—"

Morgan is on her feet, rising into the stench. The noise of an approaching engine means the arrival of the first of the day's cattle liners full of hogs. The rig is turning, slowing, moving into the parking lot, bending and straightening until it is perfectly aligned, moving steadily backward, like a beam sinking into the open eye of a loading bay door. The steel walls of the cattle trailer are not solid sheets of metal. They are cut open all over with square and rectangular vents, something like a sturdy, rigid mesh. The early morning light is strong enough to show movements through the vents, the pale hairy sides of hogs pressed against the trailer walls—tails and rooting snouts, sprays of feces dried like plaster to the metal. The truck's back up alarm bleats into the dawn.

The chugging of the diesel engine cuts when there is no more space between the truck's rear bumper and the entrance to the factory. Morgan takes two steps closer, hoping to see more. There is a padding of hoofs on foam-covered floors, animal grunts, men's voices. There is no squealing panic, no shouting, no hissing hellfire. It is not a stampede, but a march.

Light from inside the Freibergs receiving bay shines through the trailer's vents. If she were to get close enough to press her face against the trailer, Morgan might be able to see the hogs walking themselves into the slaughter-house. She lifts one foot to step over the concrete curb, leaving the grassy ground where she and Paul have been sitting.

"Wait." Paul has leaned forward to grab at her sleeve, flicking her arm backward, tossing it high enough to catch it and take hold of her hand. "Wait," he says. "I don't like it. Don't go."

She turns. The sun is rising behind him, blackening his face. In silhouette, he is a dark broken head, a net of warm fingers closed around her hand, the high, sweet voice that calls her back.

12

One week before Brett Finnemore's homicide trial begins,
Morgan looks again for the old television footage of Reverend Len Vreend exorcising the Chinook Hockey Arena.
She has searched the Internet on her own laptop, and now
on the computers at the public library, in case their algo-
rithms have developed differently and the results change.

> Vreend shooting exorcism
> Vreend shooting
> Vreend evil

The term "Vreend prayer" is the most fruitful, bringing
Morgan to archived newspaper stories written by reporters who sat in the arena during Vreend Junior's memorial
service. It is something but it's not the video record she
wanted. That is gone—not preserved on a VHS tape, left
sitting at the back of a cabinet in someone's living room,
uploaded years later—just gone. She reads to the end of
the first news story twice before finding the note printed in faint blue italics at the bottom of the page. It con-
fesses that editing had been done since the story was first

printed, but it does not confess where or how. Morgan knows without being told. Reverend Vreend is still quoted saying, "Evil has entered this place, and it must be sent out" but the word "exorcism" has vanished from the electronic copies of the newspapers. When even the word vanishes, does that mean an exorcism is a success—or an utter failure?

It is not gone without a trace. There is a new phrase in the articles, set where "exorcism" should have been. Reverend Vreend, the articles say, performed "a rite to reclaim the arena." Saying it in these words is not strictly wrong, but it is not right. Cheated out of the only exorcism she has ever witnessed, Morgan closes the browser, stands up under the library's fluorescent lights. Is the edited story right enough to make her wrong about what she has always believed she saw on television that day? The still pictures in the news stories have no answer, not even on Reverend Vreend's face—his mouth is open, maybe in the very act of saying the word devil, saying evil, saying the words to cast it out of all recorded history.

Morgan leaves the library's computers, heading into the stacks. If she can't read what Vreend said in the newspaper anymore, maybe the same words are in the Bible somewhere. He must have learned them there. She finds a shelf jammed with Bibles—thick ones heavy as furniture and written in King James English, hip paperbacks decorated in the style of basketball shoes. One of them looks more familiar to her than the rest. It is thin, bound in a hard red cover embossed with a gold water pitcher, or maybe it's a lamp made to burn slippery liquid fuel.

It's a selection of the New Testament only, the easy parts, the Jesus parts. The print is large, as if it's meant for school children. She scans the pages but there are too many demons, too many swine. She takes the red book back to the computers, where she can make a proper search. The devils and the pigs appear first on the screen and then in the book, just as Paul Lund said they would. There are no magic words, no tools. God just tells the devils to go away.

It won't work for her. Morgan is no god, just a person—not even a churchy person. She was never taught these stories, let alone what she should do with them. She carries the Bible away, forces it back into its place on the shelf. It is not the instruction manual she hoped it would be, but there is still one more resource left for her to consult in the library: the DVD movie section. This is where she finds a shelf packed with different versions of *The Exorcist*—sequels, prequels, director's cut, extended director's cut, international editions. Morgan chooses the original film made before she was born.

At home, alone in her room, she watches it, intent on writing down every ceremonial word the Hollywood clerics speak to the crusty green demon. The actors aren't real priests, of course, but they must be closer to actual professional priests than a psychotic, lapsed Mormon, former missionary telling stories in a parking lot. The movie exorcists have a uniform, weaponized icons, words that aren't their own to speak in a Swedish accent to the devil's face. They scream but don't cry. None of it matters. In the end, the film's story breaks down into relics gone wrong, punching, gagging, falling. It's dark and useless.

Where would a devil be, anyways? He wouldn't be in jail with Finnemore. No, at this point Finnemore is a hog drowned in the sea, wasted meat, as far as a devil would be concerned—shackled, sedated, spent. The ending credits of *The Exorcist* are still rolling when Morgan closes her laptop, pulls the earbuds out of her head, looks at her bedroom reflected in the dark glass of her window in deep purple and lightbulb-coloured gold. What, she asks herself, is the most devilish thing in her mother's house? What would a devil possess if he was here?

She knows. Morgan steps into the hallway. It's Tod's week to work the night shift on the Freibergs scalder. His bedroom is quiet and empty, unguarded. She turns on the light and crosses the carpet to the dusty rack of music CDs Tod collected when they were younger. They are disused but still here, still alphabetized, descending in order toward the floor, toward the letter S. This is where she finds the longtime resident demons of Tod's room, the ones who will be the first subjects of Morgan's experimental exorcism—the practice one that won't matter. They are burned into Tod's collection of Skinny Puppy CDs—an early electronic goth band made up of two guys named Kevin with ghoulish stage personae. Morgan first heard their music on dubbed cassette tapes—the only media that would play in Tod's high school car. Wherever Sheila made him drive her, they traveled without conversation, in a clamour of shrieks and synthesizers. Only once did she ask him to change the tape.

"What? You're lucky to know anything about them, Morgo," he called over the music. "Skinny Puppy is genius. They wrote and recorded this years before Nine Inch Nails—ages before Marilyn Manson and Rob Zombie and all that American trash."

Standing in Tod's room tonight, she can only call the chorus of one of the old songs to mind. The details of the rest are gone, but the sense remains—the memory of the music as distorted and furious about something like the environment or capitalism or maybe just about being alone. The voices, sound effects, costumes and artwork—all of it was uncanny, at once human and not human. Morgan slides each of the Skinny Puppy CDs out of the wire rack, her fingerprints leaving clear streaks and ovals in the layer of dust on the plastic cases. Pall of dust—here and now, call it a pall.

The real Reverend Vreend had only a Bible during his exorcism. The movie exorcists added the drama of crosses and holy water. Anyone can buy a cross at a jewelry counter. Morgan knows that. She does not know what makes water holy. Do priests fabricate it from scratch, distilling it out of the air in dank church basements, or do they consecrate their tap-water as it comes out of the wall? Maybe holy water distribution is centralized and controlled—something that can be ordered on the Internet but only if properly authorized.

Wherever it comes from, there is no holy water in Tod's bedroom. There is, however, Dreamweaver3000. At the bottom of its hydration reservoir is a centimetre of lukewarm water—the source of the fine mist that, just a few hours ago, while he lay day-sleeping, was blown through the air piped into Tod's respiratory system to keep his body from smothering itself. Maybe there isn't anything holier for water to do.

Tod's collection contains Skinny Puppy's entire discography. It is far more than Morgan needs. She will choose only one CD, selecting it based on nothing but its cover art—heavily filtered images of skeletons, horror movie gore, small bare breasts. One of the singles is different, marked with artwork she has come to know well. It is something old, lifted from the public domain so the record company wouldn't have to pay for it. The image is a scene from Dante's *Inferno*—again, even here. It is an engraving of a soul in hell, upright in an open grave, naked, of course, burning, of course—not rotten but gaunt. Virgil and Dante stand on the uneven ground above it, deep enough into the cantos to not be cringing in horror anymore.

Morgan sets the CD on the bedside table, beside Dreamweaver3000. She slides the reservoir out of the machine, wets the end of the index finger of her right hand, holds the drooping drop of homemade holy water over Skinny Puppy's reproduction of the picture of the open grave in hell. If this is enough, if the exorcism is done correctly, she will know when she plays the disc after she's finished. There will be no more screaming, no moaning left on the track.

The drop of water on Morgan's fingertip hangs, wavers but doesn't fall. She bends closer to it, doesn't see herself reflected in it, just a section of the wall behind her, upside down. The water waits for something more—something from her. If she were a movie exorcist, it would be a cue to yell or chant. What is there to say? Maybe she should have borrowed the library's Bibles after all.

The drop of water still hasn't fallen when the yelling starts on its own. "Morgo—what the hell?"

Tod stands in his bedroom doorway. Morgan jerks to a straighter posture, saying nothing. They aren't kids anymore. There will be no fighting, no appealing to Sheila for justice or retribution for this trespass. Tod blows out a long breath, clockwork grinding. Morgan finally stammers something about wanting to check the water level in Dreamweaver3000. She mashes past him in the doorway, turning hard, closing herself into her own bedroom.

Tod accepts this infraction, tucks it away with the rest of the things that make no sense, that are too bad about the way Morgan has grown up. He walks to the bedside table to find the cellphone charger he needs to make it through the rest of the night shift. While he coils the cord into his pocket, he jams the displaced reservoir back into the CPAP machine. He hasn't handled a Skinny Puppy CD in years but there's one now, on the tabletop. He lifts it close to his face, trying to remember why he ever bought this one. It's a single of a song he already owned on an album. Maybe it was just for the artwork. It's pretty classy for Puppy album art. The case is wet. He flicks it to shake the water off the plastic before it rolls inside the case to dampen and curl the paper. Light and slippery, the entire case flies out of Tod's fingers. The flimsy plastic square spins sideways through the open door of his closet, cracking as its thin, brittle hinges break against the wall. The case and its contents fall to pieces behind the laundry hamper, into moist darkness.

There is no time for any of this—Morgan and her morbid games. There's a real world to be lived in, one where the clock on Tod's break time is running out. If he doesn't leave the house now, he won't make it back to Freibergs in time to punch back in without a penalty. He turns, leaves, forgets, and the disc is lost.

13

Passing from pre-trial time to the time of a trial proper is not like scaling a mountain and arriving at its summit, or making any other graded, controlled progression. Instead, it is like moving from standing in the open door in the side of an airplane—winds and engines roaring and tearing at everything—to jumping out into freefall, racing toward an uncertain end at terminal velocity, falling but with the sensation of hanging, helpless.

Down we go.

The trial of Brett Marshall Finnemore at the Court of Queen's Bench for second degree murder and offering an indignity to a dead body is underway. There will be no more delay—no adjournments, no new lawyers, nothing. The inflight movie for these four weeks of freefall is, of course, a horror movie—Tricia Turner's horror movie, the part after the ending, the credits, the long list of who did what that scrolls on and on, white letters almost too small to read on a vast black screen.

If Morgan bore any kind of sisterly resemblance to Tricia, maybe she would sit on the groom's side of the courtroom, in the front row closest to the prisoner's dock where Brett Finnemore might look up and see her. She would powder her face, hide her hair in a black cowl, and stare straight ahead, as if this time, she is unknowing. A white cowl might be better. It really is a shame the wedding dress is buried. Morgan wouldn't have worn it but maybe, folded into a bag, the courthouse sheriffs would have let her bring it through security, drape it over a chair at the front of the gallery, just behind the bar.

No, there has been none of that—no shrouds, no stunts inside the courtroom. All of this has been in Morgan's mind but in the flesh, she has simply taken her seat with the rest of her family on the bride's side. One hand in her hair, she vacantly pulls hanks of it across her face—a new habit—sniffing to see if it smells like hogs. It doesn't, not yet.

Sheila Turner and her surviving children are in the courtroom listening to the testimony of the woman who was working the drive-thru window the night Finnemore drove Tricia's car sanely and safely through the lane to get his refreshing post-murder coffee. Endless police officers testify—those who handled the forensic investigations at Tricia's apartment, on the lawn outside, in her car, in the impromptu boneyard outside Innisfail. There are the officers who arrested Finnemore at the gas-well site in Saskatchewan, the ones who processed him in remand. Finally, they hear from the star police witness, the detective who sat with Finnemore in an interview room for four-and-a-half hours, through the storytelling about demons in Tricia's head, all the way to the confession. On the video recording of the interview, the court hears Finnemore say in his own voice, through his own tears, that he killed Tricia and drove away with her body.

The stream of medical witnesses begins with the psychiatric nurses and social workers who have worked with Finnemore since his arrest. There is his doctor who treated his mental illnesses before the murder and, last of all in the prosecution's case, a psychiatrist, an expert witness who supports the Crown's version of events, where Brett Finnemore was aware that Tricia Turner was being murdered and defiled when he bludgeoned her, when he threw her off a balcony, when he abandoned her in a field. Finnemore knew it was wrong to kill people. He understood as well as anyone can what it means to put a violent end to someone else's life. When the killing was over, he had the insight to see he was in trouble and made calculating, callous choices to preserve himself.

"When he's on his medication, Mr. Finnemore is not acutely psychotic. But he is always a psychopath. Psychotic, psychopath—I understand the terminology is confusing," the psychiatrist apologizes. "We'll often use the term 'antisocial personality disorder' rather than 'psychopath' but they mean the same thing. Mr. Finnemore could have an antisocial personality disorder and still have understood what he was doing and that it was wrong when he killed Ms. Turner. Someone suffering from acute psychosis might not be able to understand that, but someone with an antisocial personality disorder would—he just wouldn't care. That's what we're dealing with here."

According to all of this, Brett Finnemore is guilty of

second degree murder and offering an indignity to a dead body, and he must be held criminally responsible for it. From opening arguments until his case was finished, this is what Joshua Lund has said as many times as he could, in every way he could.

The defence case is broader, loose. Dean Orenchuk's witnesses are Finnemore's parents, ex-girlfriends, ex-friends—anyone who has ever known him to do anything demented before or since the murder. Yes, he was a monster of a teenager, a bully of a boyfriend, he never kept a job more than a few weeks, we had horrible fights. Yes, we were afraid of him. Yes, everyone else was afraid for us. No, the fact that we loved him didn't make any difference. Yes, he is beautiful, charming, and always, always insane.

Defence argues that the most specific and timely testimony is that of a neighbour of Tricia's, a man who passed Finnemore in the foyer of her apartment building the day the murder may have happened. "I never liked the look of him. But that night, he was different, all glassy-eyed and empty—I don't know, the sight of him freaked me out a bit."

An expert witness needs to be called in order for defence to answer the opinion offered by the prosecution's expert witness about Finnemore's state of mind in the moment he killed Tricia. They have found one in Dr. Ian Hale, a psychiatrist who supports a version of events where Brett Finnemore suffered from psychotic delusions serious enough to keep him from understanding that killing Tricia was wrong. In his mind, Brett Finnemore was destroying a Satanic force, not a living human.

He was good triumphing over evil.

Dueling expert witnesses—it's the main event of any Not Criminally Responsible defence. That's what Coleen told the Turners.

Josh told Gillian the same. She is here today, sitting in the gallery, on the defence side, making notes between grinning, nodding, sneering, silently laughing and scoffing, pantomiming for the jury so they will know how they should feel about whatever they hear. She passed Morgan in the waiting room, before the sheriffs unlocked the courtroom for the day. She clasped Morgan's hand, hidden in their sleeves.

"It's fine. It's going to be fine."

The noon recess has ended, and Dr. Hale is on the witness stand again. He has hit his stride, no more stiff overly formal nerves after testifying in-direct all morning—telling his story without being challenged on its truthfulness, the defence lawyer laying down polite questions for him to pick up and present to the jury. They have entered the doctor's curriculum vitae into the record—the details of his medical training and experience. He is a specialist physician, not some psychologist. He has a prescription pad, hospital privileges and, for a change of pace and to fulfill his sense of civic duty, he occasionally consults in criminal matters like Brett Finnemore's homicide trial. Tomorrow, his name will be in every newspaper in the province.

It is time for Dr. Ian Hale to face the prosecution. Joshua Lund stands, rising in his robe like a black shade in front of the bar. "Dr. Hale, psychological stress can be scaled, can't it? Some stressors are recognized as much more damaging than others, would you agree?"

Dr. Hale nods, tipping the shiny top of his head toward the gallery. "Yes."

Josh waves at the jury. "Just to be clear, this means the stress of losing your car keys would have nowhere near the psychological impact on a person as the stress of, say, hurting a loved one. Is that correct?"

"If one is healthy enough to understand the differences between a set of keys and a loved one then, yes, that is correct."

"Yes, and traumatic stressors can be damaging enough to get psychiatric conditions to flare up, say, like the psychotic state in which you found Mr. Finnemore when you met him for the first time in Alberta Hospital Edmonton?"

Dr. Hale frowns. "Not Mr. Finnemore in particular, no. But it is possible to have that kind of response to stress. Generally speaking, yes, stress can affect a psychotic disorder in negative ways."

"A psychotic disorder such as Brett Finnemore's paranoid schizophrenia?"

"As I just said, no, not in Brett Finnemore."

Joshua Lund folds his arms over his chest. "I'm trying to understand why you say not Mr. Finnemore in particular. Does he, unlike most everyone else not respond to stress? Does his case fall outside normal, generalizable psychiatric patterns? You've been qualified as an expert in psychiatric medicine so we're going to have a problem if you're not inclined to make statements about general patterns of mental illness."

Dr. Hale rolls his shoulders. "I am certainly qualified. However, every case 'falls outside normal' to some extent."

"So certain elements of Mr. Finnemore's case—which we can discuss in detail shortly—mean we can't proceed here as if he has much in common with most other schizophrenia patients. Is that fair to say?"

Dr. Hale glances at Dean Orenchuk. "It's a bit strong."

Josh is nodding. "*A bit* strong. We'll move on for now. Back to stress. Intense stress can make a treatment that used to work, stop working. Would you agree with that?"

"In general, I would agree. But not in Mr. Finnemore's case. I'm not sure where you're heading."

Josh smiles. "No need to worry about what's ahead. You can relax and take each question as it comes. Would you agree, Dr. Hale, that in order to assess the effects that the stress of killing Tricia Turner had on Mr. Finnemore, you would need to compare his mental health before the killing to his mental health after the killing?"

"Yes, and as I testified this morning, Mr. Finnemore had a long history of very troubled mental health before Ms. Turner's death. She didn't deserve what happened to her but she did choose as her romantic partner a man well-known to be very sick. It's a risk she knew and accepted."

Josh takes a step forward. "Sir, Tricia Turner's judgment is not on trial."

"No, of course not, but—what I am saying is, as is typical among people diagnosed with paranoid schizophrenia, Mr. Finnemore has been in treatment since he was a teenager. His ill health is well-documented and well-known. Defence counsel and I just entered all of that into evidence."

"Yes, it's all been entered, along with a report made during an in-patient hospital stay during his early twenties wherein Mr. Finnemore was diagnosed with an antisocial personality disorder. You're familiar with that aspect of Mr. Finnemore's condition, aren't you?"

"Yes."

"But you didn't factor the effects of Mr. Finnemore's antisocial personality disorder into your analysis of his fatal attack on Ms. Turner, did you? You never mentioned it in your testimony this morning nor in your written reports to the court, not once."

"Look, many people have concurrent, overlapping psychiatric conditions. Antisocial personality disorders are often co-morbid with schizophrenia. We don't have to choose between diagnosing one or the other. Brett Finnemore has an antisocial personality disorder and schizophrenia, which is a psychotic disorder that impairs his ability to understand the world around him."

Josh waits, nods. "That combination of psychiatric conditions sounds like a dangerous cocktail. You've said even someone who wasn't a mental health professional—someone like Tricia Turner—should have been able to see that. So as someone appearing in this court as an expert testifying about Brett Finnemore's psychiatric profile, it's strange that you only referred to half of it this morning, isn't it?"

It is not actually a question. Dr. Hale answers anyway. "No, it's not strange to omit irrelevant material during a court proceeding. I mean, if Brett had gallstones I would not mention them here either. Just because he has a condition doesn't mean it's involved in the crime. No, what's relevant is his psychotic disorder, an illness I did testify about at length."

Josh inhales deeply enough for everyone to hear. "Let's try this again. Was Brett Finnemore's antisocial personality disorder factored into your analysis of his brutal attack on Ms. Turner? Was it, or was it not?"

"It was. It was considered and then dismissed. I don't understand why this is so challenging for you."

"Yes, I am struggling here. Please help me, Dr. Hale. As far as I can tell, an antisocial personality disorder wouldn't prevent a patient from understanding that a psychiatric sentence can be shorter and more comfortable than a penitentiary sentence. And with that understanding, the patient might be motivated to work toward getting a psychiatric sentence even if it meant changing his story or even of willfully quitting his medications in order to make a better case for the kind of sentence he'd prefer—the kind he would serve in a hospital instead of—"

Dean Orenchuk stands. "M'lady, Crown Counsel has not been qualified as a psychiatric expert himself and I must object to him giving testimony as one."

"Yes, Mr. Lund," the judge agrees, "do you have a question for Dr. Hale along these lines or not?"

Josh clears his throat. "Excuse me, M'lady. My question is, in light of the propensity for deception and cunning that goes with an antisocial personality disorder, how was it so easily dismissed in the analysis of Mr. Finnemore? Dr. Hale, please explain how an illness like this becomes irrelevant to our proceedings."

"It's irrelevant because it didn't matter. In the matter before this court, it was the psychotic disorder, the schizophrenia, driving the bus."

"Bus," Josh echoes. "Dr. Hale, from what I've seen and heard, there was no real basis for your dismissal of Brett Finnemore's profound and pervasive antisocial personality disorder. You dismissed it in error, as an oversight, didn't you?"

"My basis for dismissing it was my status as an expert in psychiatric medicine. I dismissed it based on my twenty-five years of clinical experience working with deeply disturbed individuals day in and day out."

"Thank you, sir, your qualifications have already been entered into evidence. What I need now is for you to elaborate on a single clinical decision you made to dismiss a large portion of Brett Finnemore's psychiatric condition: his antisocial personality disorder. You overlooked it, didn't you? You made a mistake. Isn't that right?"

"Look, by the time I met Brett, his psychotic disorder had completely disconnected him from reality. He was deluded and actively hallucinating. His schizophrenia was out of control. It had eclipsed all other pathologies."

"Out of control." Josh begins again. "Yes, let's return to Mr. Finnemore's other well-documented, longstanding psychiatric disorder—the one he has in addition to his antisocial personality disorder, his schizophrenia. In the past, it has been well-treated, would you agree?"

"I haven't treated Mr. Finnemore myself. I've only assessed him."

"And in that assessment, you would have seen the notes of doctors and social workers and psychologists who did treat him over the years, isn't that so?"

"Of course."

"And according to your review of Brett Finnemore's medical records, do you find that his treatment for schizophrenia—his medications, counselling, therapies, hospital stays—was appropriate?"

"Every physician is going to favour slightly different approaches."

"So his treatment was mishandled, in your view?"

"No, it—I'd appreciate it if you'd let me finish a thought." There is a long pause as Dr. Hale waits for something obsequious to urge him on.

Josh nods, not at all a bow. "Please, continue. Please give us your opinion of the appropriateness of Brett Finnemore's anti-psychotic medications in the months leading up to his killing of Tricia Turner."

"The doses seem well-conceived on paper but psychiatric medications require fine-tuning on an individual basis in order to be beneficial."

"So medications of this kind can work differently for different people?"

"Yes. It's very individual."

"And their effectiveness can change over time?"

"Yes, definitely."

"Would you say Mr. Finnemore saw his doctor frequently enough to allow his doctor to respond to changes in his medication needs?"

"I don't now recall."

Josh flips to a page in the huge binder of paper exhibits on the table in front of him. "That's alright, we can look it up. Earlier in the month of Tricia Turner's murder, Mr. Finnemore went to his scheduled check-up with his doctor at the downtown mental health clinic. He made no complaints, reported feeling reasonably well and stable, and did not require any changes in his psychoactive medications. He was given a prescription for some acid reflux but other than that, the treatment team's plan was to stay the course."

"May I see that?"

Josh turns the binder over to the doctor, tells the judge and jury which page to refer to in their books. The doctor nods. "Yes, that does seem to be what is noted here."

"Seems to be?"

"Is—it is what they have written here."

"Yes. So, we've established Mr. Finnemore was a paranoid schizophrenic with an antisocial personality disorder who reported to his doctor during their final visit before killing Ms. Turner that his psychotic condition was stable and properly treated. Would you agree?"

"I just did. On the day he saw his doctor, someone made a note of him saying he was fine."

"Maybe you can help us read this medical chart, Dr. Hale. Where can we find the names of the drugs Brett Finnemore has been prescribed to treat his antisocial personality disorder?"

Dr. Hale shakes his head. "You won't find any. None. There are no such drugs."

"So this antisocial personality disorder, it can't be medically treated and it never goes away?"

"Counselling can sometimes help, cognitive therapy and all of that—but as of now there are no approved drug treatments."

Josh taps his index finger against his own jaw. "Does an antisocial personality disorder keep people from understanding their actions, from knowing that the society they live in considers certain things wrong—criminal?"

"A personality disorder is not considered a psychotic disorder, if that's what you're getting at. You can have a disorder like that and still understand what's real—unless, like Brett Finnemore, you've also got a raging psychotic disorder. That's completely different."

"Completely different, yes." Josh scrawls something on a curling yellow notepad. "Yes, back to Brett Finnemore's medical care. The day he last saw his doctor before his arrest—when was that? Can I trouble you to read the date from the medical chart exhibit?"

"It says March 7, 2014."

"About three weeks before he killed Tricia Turner."

"Yes. So I see here."

"Three weeks. And when was it you met Mr. Finnemore at the hospital after his arrest, Dr. Hale?"

"December 2014."

"Roughly nine months after he killed Ms. Turner. So these notes were taken by a doctor who knew Mr. Finnemore as a patient quite well and close in time to the murder. You may not be aware that this doctor has been here and testified during the Crown case. His observations must reflect a more accurate picture of Mr. Finnemore's mental state at the time he killed Ms. Turner than observations made months and months later, wouldn't they?"

Dr. Hale hands the exhibit binder to the court clerk over the wall of the witness stand. "I see what you're doing. Timing isn't the only consideration in interpolating state of mind. When I met Mr. Finnemore he was in a terrible condition—one brought on by a previous psychotic break and a complete meltdown in his psychiatric condition."

"Yes. What could have brought on that kind of thing?"

Dr. Hale coughs. "He could have stopped taking his medications. That's usually how it happens. I believe he was un-medicated when arrested." He waves at the exhibit on the clerk's desk. "Isn't there something in all of that about it? I remember seeing it in the notes."

Josh answers. "Yes, you're remembering correctly. At the time of arrest, in May 2014, two months after Ms. Turner's death, Mr. Finnemore was no longer taking his medications. But why would he do that—stop taking his pills?"

"I don't know. No one knows. It's an ongoing problem across mental health services users. No one can say precisely why any of them do it. But it happens all the time. Who knows?"

"Are we to understand that you haven't asked Brett Finnemore when or why he discontinued his medication? You aren't able to testify in particular about it?"

"I can't answer from first hand clinical knowledge. But his tragic outburst shows his illness was out of control at the time of Ms. Turner's death which strongly suggests he'd discontinued his medication before then."

"Suggests?"

"The truth is, at the time of the incident, Brett's behaviour was clearly, violently psychotic—not at all stable, no matter what he told his doctor. It's obvious."

Josh's finger is tapping against his jaw again. "The truth is we have a bit of a chicken-egg problem before us, don't we? Mr. Finnemore is in the difficult position of needing to convince the court that he fell mentally ill and then killed Tricia Turner. Otherwise, according to the law, the court must accept a version of events where he was not psychotic when he killed Tricia Turner, but relapsed into his old illness afterward, for whatever reason—perhaps due to the stress of beating her to death, or perhaps even as a cunning—"

Dean Orenchuk is standing, addressing the judge. "M'Lady, I must say I'm taken aback hearing Crown Counsel inviting Dr. Hale to speculate on a matter of legal argument outside his psychiatric expertise."

"Yes, back to medical testimony, please," the judge agrees.

It's useless. Dr. Hale ignores Orenchuk's objection, ignores the judge's ruling. He must scold Joshua Lund. "Listen, whatever it looks like, no matter how you twist it, we have before us one of the most disturbed individuals I have ever encountered as a forensic psychiatrist. If Not Criminally Responsible by reason of mental disease doesn't apply to him, I'm not sure what it's for."

"Thank you, Dr. Hale," Josh says. "We've been directed to return to the details your medical observations. Let's talk about how psychological stressors are often scaled."

"Fine."

"Tell us please, what type of life event is considered most stressful?"

Dr. Hale frowns. "You're about to refer to those old Holmes and Rahe stress inventory tables like you would have found in your undergraduate psychology textbooks. Those are fifty years old."

"And therefore useless?"

"No, but—they're not what you think they are. Today there is a large, complex body of psychiatric knowledge on stress and mental health."

"To be sure. But whichever measure you use, the death of a loved one is typically rated as supremely stressful, would you agree?"

Dr. Hale removes his glasses, rubs his eyes. "Sure."

"And in your opinion, would using one's own hands to cause of the death of a loved one make that stress even more intense, more dangerous to mental health?"

He folds his glasses and puts them into the pocket of his jacket. "Yeah, why not. Yes."

"Could this kind of stress explain a 'complete meltdown' in someone's psychiatric condition, like the one you've described in Mr. Finnemore after the murder? Could killing Tricia Turner be the cause of Mr. Finnemore's psychotic break?"

"Which question do you want me to answer? In this situation, the tragic death happened as a result of acute psychosis. Brett wasn't as stressed by the murder as you or I would be because he doesn't understand that it was wrong."

"I want you to answer both questions. You've answered the question of whether you think Mr. Finnemore's mental health was affected by killing Ms. Turner. Now answer my first question, please. Answer the question of whether—regardless of the conclusion you've come to in this case—could it have been *possible* for Mr. Finnemore to have suffered a psychotic break *after* killing Ms. Turner, one brought on by the trauma of killing her knowing it was wrong. Are you saying it's impossible for that to have been the case? Was it impossible or possible? Is it possible?"

"It's *not* what happened."

"With respect, sir, you were not there the moment Brett Finnemore shattered Tricia Turner's skull with a table lamp. Please tell us as a dispassionate psychiatrist, *could* such an act bring on a psychotic break?"

Dr. Hale glances at Orenchuk, at Finnemore,

sleepy in the dock. He says, "Sure. Sure, anything's possible. Anything can happen. Why not make that the answer for everything here? Anything can happen. How's that? Can I get a chair?"

The cross-examination goes on and on. Read it as it happened—slow, slow rejoinders staggered between long, tense pauses, the flipping of paper and shuffling of binders. Read it as a TV courtroom drama, only in slow motion, with the volume low and muffled, the dead air unedited.

Josh finishes with Dr. Hale, the trial is in a recess again, and not to give anyone a rest. When the floor was returned to Dean Orenchuk to finish the defence case, he stood up and said something that had Josh on his feet again, objecting. It was fast and technical. No one seemed to understand what was going on except for the judge and both of the lawyers. She sent the jury away and told the lawyers to confer and report back to the courtroom in thirty minutes.

The most frantic moments of the trial happen during the breaks, in the courthouse briefing offices. Closed inside one of these small rooms, Joshua Lund is standing across a table from Dean Orenchuk, trying not to shout. "You cannot raise the issue of 'Tunnel Vision' in a trial where you've already agreed to plead guilty and we're just arguing about criminal responsibility due to mental disease, for crying out loud. It makes no sense."

"Well, Josh, that's where we disagree."

"Dean, either I'm professionally incompetent or I understand that Tunnel Vision means the prosecutors or police purposely ignored evidence that doesn't support our theory and have doggedly chased down the wrong person. But you've admitted almost everything in the investigation except for your client's state of mind. The *actus reus* is settled. All we've got to argue about is *mens rea*. Am I wrong? I can't be. What other evidence is there of Finnemore's state of mind besides what we've both put forward? What has been willfully ignored?"

Orenchuk fans his torso with the wings of his long black robe. "All I'm saying is, I'm deeply troubled that you won't seriously and properly consider the issue of mental illness in your prosecution, and I worry it's interfering with Brett Finnemore's access to a fair trial."

"I cannot imagine what you mean by that. What hasn't been 'properly considered?' We called our medical and expert psychiatric witnesses; you called yours. Each of them carefully considered nothing but the issue of mental illness and each was thoroughly examined about it in-direct and in cross-exam just now. That's all there is. That's the procedure. Be specific: what more do you want?"

"Joshua—the problem is you don't believe in mental illness. You see it as a lame excuse and you consistently oppose NCR defences on principle, the way you did with the motorhome arsonist earlier this year."

"The arsonist?"

Orenchuk lifts a printed copy of the judgment of the arson trial out of his briefcase, tosses it onto the table. "You've established a pattern of Tunnel Vision when it comes to NCR defences. Your judgment is confounded by your frustration with your brother's misfortunes in the mental health diversion programme. Yes, we can produce a record of his court matters too. How can you say none of it affects your practice?"

Josh sits heavily on the edge of the table, laughing quietly, the fingers of one hand pressed against his forehead.

Orenchuk crashes into the breach. "Look, I'm sorry to have to bring it up, but it's on the public record. Your brother's name was lit up on the monitors by the main doors downstairs, for God's sake. Your sister was seen down at the case management office pulling on his arm, jumping up and down, just barely keeping him under control. It was frightening and ugly."

"What? When did you see that? When did you see anything like that?"

"I have it on good authority."

"Who saw it? Who saw my brother barely under control anywhere in this building at any time?"

"Dana Randall saw it."

Josh laughs again—loudly now.

"Now Josh, I know she and Mitch are no friends of yours but Dana is an officer of the court with all the integrity that implies." He is nearly shouting to make himself heard over Josh's horrible laughter. "She says she couldn't help but notice your brother's disturbance at the counter. He must be gravely ill. And it seemed like your sister was extremely frustrated—almost abusive toward him. I'm told it was quite a scene. And it's not that I blame your sister. A sick family member has got to be a terrible burden on all of you. I can understand how you might feel subconsciously vindicated by acting out your passive aggression toward your brother on a soft, captive target like Brett Finnemore."

Josh bellows more laughter.

Orenchuk goes on. "I'm saying it's raised concerns for me and now, I'm bound to raise them in Finnemore's defence. That's what he deserves. I don't want to make this personal but we're dealing with your demonstrated inability to make a fair consideration of mental health factors in prosecutions. We need to let you out of this, let you step aside and deal with your demons, and bring in a prosecutor who can settle this in a fair manner."

Josh has stopped laughing. "You disrupted court and brought me in here to threaten to put me and my family on trial."

Orenchuk sits at the table. "Come down out of cross-exam mode and let's find some common ground. Let's work together. If we can agree on a few things there's no need for any of this."

"You are trying to intimidate me into giving up and giving in and joining you in asking the court to go ahead and find Finnemore NCR so I can protect vulnerable people I care about from getting dragged into this. Is that it Dean? How's your family, Dean? Everyone okay? No one ever been on any happy pills? Seems like a bit of a stretch nowadays. I'm sure we could find some sad, hapless patient back at your place and make this process into a complete circus, trigger a mistrial, buy your boy Finnemore some time to log toward a Section 11(b) application to have these charges dropped for an unconstitutional delay of proceedings. The courts have done it before, even with murder trials. Is that it? Are you working at keeping this thing lolling around in the courts long enough to have it thrown out for violating Finnemore's right to a speedy trial? We're already years into this—looks pretty good."

"Josh, we want this over as badly as you do—worse. It's not until the trial is over that Brett can get out of remand and start to heal and get his life back."

Josh stands. "No worries, Dean. I won't involve your family. You know why? Because I don't care. As you're well aware, the issue of our family members' mental health is completely irrelevant. You go ahead, you open a *voir dire*, stand up in front of the judge, and bring whatever half-baked motion you like against me. Give it a try. Keep making all of this up as you go along. Meanwhile, we will be right there answering with the law—stacks of cases—showing you have no basis to make these arguments in front of the jury, exposing your case for having no real defence. You want to negotiate? At this point, this is my final offer, Dean: have Brett Finnemore make a clean, unqualified guilty plea so he can start answering properly for everything he did to that woman."

Josh shoulders through the door of the briefing office, cell phone between his hands, texting Coleen. It's all gone sideways again and they're going to be up all night.

Coleen won't read Josh's text right away. In another courthouse briefing office, she is meeting with Tod,

Morgan, and Sheila.

"More *voir dires*—they're wasting time," Sheila says, "They're doing it again—having all the best hearings, doing all their best talking when the jury isn't even in the room to hear any of it."

Coleen nods. "Yes, we've had a lot of *voir dire* hearings during this trial. They're time-consuming but they give the judge a chance to preview certain kinds of evidence to make sure it's relevant and legal for the jury to hear them. Without a *voir dire*, it's easier to end up with legal problems with the evidence, and whatever verdict the jury finds could be overturned by the appeal courts. We don't want Finnemore walking away looking like some tragic poster boy for wrongful conviction."

Sheila swears, waves a hand toward Morgan. "He confessed to killing my daughter."

"Yes, we have a strong case. And Dr. Hale's cross-examination went extremely well. I think that's why Orenchuk panicked and dragged us into another *voir dire*. But we need a clean conviction from the jury or we've got nothing. And there's no other way to get one."

Sheila goes on. "So the rules let the judge hide the truth from the jury."

Coleen knows only the very angriest people invoke the truth. "Sheila," she says, "don't forget. The judge does not decide in the end. It's up to the jury—people likely to see right and wrong the same way you do. Trust them."

The meeting with Coleen ends when a courthouse runner knocks on the door to deliver a thin manila envelope. No one is offended by the interruption this time. The Turners need to get away from here, away from each other. Alone in the office, Coleen reads the letter.

Sheila and Tod leave and there is no one Morgan knows left in the hallway outside the courtroom. Gillian was here but Morgan hasn't seen her since she brushed past her in the waiting area saying, "Did you see? Really well, it's going really well."

Morgan stands by herself now. If Lilian was here, would she be able to follow the slow but complicated courtroom English? Lawyers do strange things with language. If Sheila would calm down during their meetings, maybe Morgan would remember to ask Coleen what "an information" is supposed to mean.

To attend the trial, Morgan has taken a short leave from the Freibergs dishwasher. Her last shift was the day she and the cafeteria ladies watched episode fifteen of their current Korean drama series. Episode fifteen is the point in the story where the writers usually tear down everything they've spent the previous episodes building up just so they can right it all for the finale in episode sixteen, tacking on a happy ending. It might be kissing in public, maybe a wedding with the spunky mom characters subdued, pretty as peonies in puffy *hanbok* dresses, and the second male lead coming to terms with loving the female lead with quiet, sad dignity from afar for the rest of his life. If it weren't for the patience of the other ladies watching along with her, Morgan would skip episode fifteen—cut it right out—every series, every time.

Their most recent episode fifteen was another one where an impossibly pretty actor lay writhing on the floor of the Incheon International Airport, weeping his tears and screaming, "*Kajima!*" for the lost love he would win back next week.

Morgan asked Lilian, just to be sure, if the word meant "don't go" in Korean.

Lilian nodded. "*Kajima*, don't go. Right."

Maybe it sounded the same in Chinese, as some things do.

"We don't say it that way," Lilian said. "Not like that. We say 不要离开."

At the end of the phrase, she pronounced one word in something close to a high shout, exaggerating the tones of her pronunciation to help Morgan hear them. Morgan does not know to listen for it. She does not know that her cafeteria Chinese lessons are like singing lessons. Lilian has thousands of different songs to teach her, ones that must be sung in perfect pitch in order to make any sense.

Morgan transposed the phrase into her Anglophone monotone.

Lilian shook her head. "No, no, no. Not 'boo yow lee kie.' Say 不要离开."

Morgan swallowed all the spit in her mouth. "开!"

"Yes, yes, yes. 不要离开!"

On the courthouse carpet, Morgan mouths the song again.

Coleen watches Morgan from the door of the briefing office, turning the newly delivered manila envelope between her fingers. Something in the Finnemore proceedings has changed—something besides Josh's row with Dean Orenchuk. It is not devastating to the proceedings, but it is awful anyway. When she sees that none of the Turners but Morgan remains in the waiting area, Coleen whispers "thank you" to no one in particular. She will meet with Morgan alone, pass the message to Sheila through her. It will be for the best.

Inside the office, Coleen asks Morgan to sit. "Your father," she begins. "He's filed a victim impact statement to be read if we get to the point where Mr. Finnemore is found criminally responsible and sentenced to time in jail. That's fairly normal. You'll probably write one yourself."

Morgan shrugs.

"But your father's statement," Coleen resumes, "is a rather unusual one. I thought the rest of the family should know and be prepared..."

Morgan is in the atrium, on the main floor of the courthouse, standing between a tropical plant and a white industrial bucket set beneath a leak in the skylight, where water drips from four storeys above. She is waiting for Sheila to appear at the top of the escalator from the courthouse basement and the system of tunnels leading to the rest of downtown.

"What is it, what's the problem?" Sheila says when she arrives under the lime-streaked glass.

Morgan tells her Marc wrote a letter to the court, for the sentencing. He wrote that the family is heartbroken but better off for this opportunity to grow. It's the family members' own fault if any of them can't move on, and no one else should be punished for it. He asked the court, no matter what, to just let Finnemore go.

Sheila's face blanches. She bows her head and starts to laugh.

It's okay though, Coleen says the court can't just let Finnemore go, no matter what.

"Of course not, it's not that. It's not Finnemore. It's him. Anything to get back to centre stage, eh Marc?" Sheila laughs again, heartily now. "I am going to kill him. I am going to murder your father, Morgan. Today is the day he finally gets me to kill him."

Morgan grabs at her sleeve, but Sheila steps out of her reach—clipping toward the exit to the street. Court is going to reopen soon. If Sheila goes anywhere, she will miss it.

"And it is high time I did."

From a distance, Morgan must raise her voice to call her mother back. It's embarrassing and it hurts her throat.

"Nope, I am heading out to his shack on the lake. I am going to find him, just like he wants me to. I'm going to gut him, the way he is gutting the rest of us. His nonsense isn't about Tricia," Sheila calls across the open space. "It's about himself as a great, saintly man who understands all of this on some higher, better level none of us can aspire to. I am having no more of it. Not anymore."

"Mom, don't go. Mom!"

"Goodbye, Morgan. Wish Mr. Lund loads of luck for me."

There is nothing to be said—no name she can call, no noise Morgan knows how to make that will bring her mother back. She is desperate, frantic, screaming.

"不要离开!"

Morgan has never shouted so loudly. At the noise of it, Sheila stops just short of crossing out of the courthouse security zone. Morgan is still standing in the milky afternoon light, yelling, finally overwrought enough to let herself pronounce the Chinese correctly.

"不要离开! 不要——"

She is out of breath, gasping to replace what she has wasted. Sheila Turner watches her daughter sink to her knees on the dirty floor. Morgan has covered her eyes with both of her hands, crying, bent toward the ground, speaking in tongues, every word of soap-opera-Korean she knows—for her mother, Tod, Tricia, for anyone.

"*Kajima, chebal, mianhae, saranghae, ottoke! Kajima!*"

Her speech breaks into coughing. Never since she's been fully grown has she used her vocal cords like this. She bows, choking into her knees.

"Oh, sweetheart, I am so sorry."

There are arms around Morgan's shoulders—not her mother's, not her brother's. Someone is smoothing her hair, touching her arms, kneeling beside her as the sheriffs advance, their hands on the radios clipped to their chests.

"Sorry guys. It's alright, we're okay," Gillian Lund tells

the sheriffs from the floor next to Morgan. "We're with the Finnemore trial and we're having a hard day. You can imagine. Sorry. We're going." She pulls Morgan's hands from her eyes. She says, "Hey. Hey, let's get up."

They stand together, Gillian pressing Kleenex into Morgan's hand. Morgan, looking past her tears and hair, sees the sheriffs poised around them, sees the line of law abiding citizens at the civil claims counter shuffling in place, growing in hate for the people that ripped them off and sent them in here with the yelling maniacs. Sheila is not standing in front of the exit anymore.

Gillian is pointing. "Look. There—up there."

At the top of the glass-walled staircase, watching from above is Morgan's mother. She has not left. She is here, about to turn and retake her seat at the trial.

Gillian persuades Morgan not to go back to the court-room yet. They sit on a sunken patio outside the build-ing. "Come on, you need a breather. Look at your hands shaking. You need nourishment. What did you have for lunch? Coffee? No? Good girl."

Morgan's shoulders slump away from the aluminum slats of the park bench behind her. She is not good. She is acting like a wild animal—like someone possessed.

Gillian pats her back. "You're fine. You've held up so well for so long. This was an isolated outburst, long over-due. It wasn't even on the record."

Neither of them says, "Not this time" but Gillian laughs at the unmade joke.

The metal bench beneath them is cold. Morgan shivers. Gillian doesn't have to sit with her. Morgan hates making her miss all the big moments every time they both show up for court.

"Nah, didn't you hear? They're dismissing the jury for a while. Looks like another *voir dire*. Can you believe it? That's Josh for you. Conscientious use of the *voir dire* process is pretty much his trademark. I missed what it was Orenchuk said to trigger it. I'm sure I'll hear all about it later though. No, Morgan, you picked the perfect time to need a break and a friend."

Gillian opens a bottle of vending machine apple juice and sets it next to Morgan on the bench. "Here, drink this. It's got vitamins and fibre."

Gillian opens a can of sugarless cola for herself. Morgan watches her hands, imagines reaching out and grabbing one of them, uninvited, the way Gillian touches her. If she were to examine Gillian's fingerprints, would they be scarred to vanishing, scalded away maybe not by a dishwasher but by something just as smooth and hot and clean? She can't ask to see them. Instead, she will look for a better end to the same conversation she had with Paul Lund before the trial started. She begins by asking Gillian if she is churchy.

Morgan has asked the question of a woman who was out of the house until eleven o'clock the night before, dressed in white, standing in a temple, not worshipping in the usual ways but taking her turn vacuuming carpets deep in its holy heart where nothing can be dirty and no ordinary caretaker can go. Gillian nods. "Churchy? Oh yeah, you could definitely say that."

No disclaimer, Morgan blurts the question of exorcism—has Gillian ever seen one?

Gillian doesn't hesitate either. "Gross. Heck no. That's an awful movie. You don't want to watch that, Morgan."

Not the movie. Morgan means a true exorcism, for when there's something real and bad and there's a priest and holy water.

"Oh," Gillian sings. "Right. Holy water is bunk, Morgan. If it was real it would be magic, and there's no such thing as magic. It's not like that."

Morgan leans into the back of the bench. Gillian doesn't believe in exorcisms. Movies are fiction. Paul Lund is a crazy crybaby. And the Bible is—well, who knows.

Gillian lifts her eyebrows. "I never said I don't believe in exorcism. What I said was, it's not like it is in movies. Real spiritual stuff is—it's normal, and usually pretty quiet. It'd make the worst movie. If my spiritual life was a movie, it'd mostly be me standing in the shower thinking really hard, or driving around in my car by myself, maybe getting a bit weepy."

Morgan hates it.

Gillian knows and says, "Hey, you know the Catholic Church has sainted people for doing nothing more than writing down nice thoughts, right? Showy stuff like bleeding out of your eyes—I'm pretty sure that's discouraged these days." Gillian says it even though she is no Catholic. "Look, it's not flamboyant, bloody sainthood, but I do have this." She flips her right hand to expose its palm, holds it close enough to Morgan's face for her to read it. Morgan looks to her fingerprints but Gillian is tapping the centre of her palm, between the lines, to a tiny brown mole Morgan can barely see. "How do you like that? My stigmata. That's what I get for being a virgin at my age, right?" Gillian laughs. "It doesn't bleed but it's still pretty cool, if you know how to look at it."

Gillian drops her hand, retracts it into her coat sleeve, the stigmata folded behind her fingers. She says, "I'm mostly kidding. But still, don't tell anyone I have this. I couldn't stand to hear it made fun of. When spiritual life drifts into physical life, people go nuts and start writing scriptures—that or panicky tirades trying to fight it off. Day to day spiritual life is more like—I don't know—being hungry, or in pain, or falling properly in love. Things that look like nothing on the outside—like electric pulses on brain scans. But Morgan, being hungry and in pain—those are the most real things we know, aren't they?"

Morgan presses her own hand to her stomach like she might be hungry herself.

"The bad, the dark," Gillian goes on, "the stuff we want to exorcize—most of the time it wouldn't make much of a movie either. Most of the time, evil is normal too. I mean, think of the guys upstairs in the docket courtroom, standing there in orange pajamas and chains. They're more sad than scary. They're people like us who've made terrible mistakes—familiar as anything. Easy to recognize because, we've all got some natural, selfish badness in us. It's in the dirt we're made of—it's the stuff that makes us grow. But then there's evil outside of us, gnawing away at the good things we're made of. It's alien—not a part of us at all. It tells lies meant to trick us into thinking we're strangers to each other. It's not true, and it's not us. And that means there's reason to hope that we can send it away—exorcise it, I guess, by learning to lay things down, and love each other anyway."

Gillian is lapsing into the metaphysical landscape of a lifetime of personal religious contemplation. For all of it, she hasn't told Morgan much of anything about how an exorcism ought to be done. Gillian is sitting over her can of Diet Coke, the tip of her thumb boring into the mole in her palm, her irises flicking sideways with a visitation of her vertigo. From her bag, she takes the small notebook the hospital has given her and marks the time.

Morgan watches the crown of Gillian's head bent over her vertigo journal until she snaps the notebook closed and says, "Anyways, real evil is nothing like it is in the movies."

Someone—it was Paul but Morgan will not mention his name to his sister—has told Morgan that everyone in Gillian's church is a minister. They all have duties and status.

"Oh, so you want to know how I would get rid of an evil spirit, as a church lady, a returned missionary, the once and former Soeur Lund. *Bien sûr*, I'll tell you." Gillian sits up straighter on the park bench. "Any demons who come around here are going to have to listen to me sing."

Getting nowhere, Morgan laughs, shakes her head.

Gillian speaks over her. "I would. I'd sing a song—a hymn, something that's supposed to be peaceful and sweet, you know. Probably a song I learned in my childhood when I was perfectly pure. Something with the Lord's name all through it. That should be enough."

Morgan nods at the stairwell through the glass wall. What would the man up there in the courtroom do?

Gillian smirks. "Joshua? His approach would be different, more formal, priestly even. But," she interrupts herself, "Morgan, hon, we're creeping ourselves out. You want something. What can I do? I want to help but this is getting weird."

Morgan tells Gillian about Reverend Vreend's public, televised exorcism—speaking in a fast, low stream of words, like a confession. She retells it—everything, beginning in the hockey arena when Vreend Junior was still alive. Gillian remembers the story—the fatal shooting of a high school boy in rural Canada on the tenth anniversary of Columbine. Of course she does, it was news all over the country. She remembers it with different markers than Morgan does—the name of the defence lawyer who negotiated the sweet deal for the killer, the short youth-sentence with early parole, the terms the shooter violated as soon as he was released. Exorcism is not part of the story Gillian remembers. She has not seen teenagers hooded like monks in their sweatshirts standing behind a reverend, trusting in him but too bewildered to pray along or even to keep crying as he waves his holy book and calls out the devil, as he says, "Evil has entered into this place, and it must be sent out."

By the end of Morgan's telling, what Gillian says is, "See, no holy water."

Morgan's mouth is dry, lips clicking as she tells Gillian that the newspapers lied. They went back and changed how they wrote it, years later. She tried to look it up, to see how Vreend did it, and the words had gone wrong. They didn't say 'exorcism' anymore. They didn't say 'devil' — none of it. Or maybe they never did. Maybe they never did and Morgan never understood. She doesn't understand anything. She doesn't know anything. She doesn't know.

Gillian is nodding, shushing again. "Hold my bag," she says, taking her laptop computer from it, pushing the rest of it into Morgan's lap. "It's not the kind of thing people brag about, but I've got librarian-level research skills. Don't let anyone tell you grad school is good for nothing."

She flexes her fingers like the token hacker character in a spy movie. "My brother, Joshua Lund, has two known flaws. The first is that he has a persistent mental block against all usernames and passwords. The second is that he writes his on sticky-notes where unauthorized people who want access to the courthouse Wi-fi can find them. Now, how do you spell Vreend?"

The spell, the spelling is spoken. It isn't long before Gillian finds the story in an index of newspaper article titles. The full text of the original isn't available anymore, but they don't need it. The headline comes from an old *Edmonton Journal* that ended up on the wire service and disseminated all over the country before it was edited. In the original version of the reporting of Len Vreend's most famous prayer, the index-only version which escaped editing is titled "Exorcising the Devil."

Gillian sets her computer on Morgan's lap, tilts the screen to clear the glare. "Look. Look, it's even better than I expected. You knew all along, Morgan. You know."

Morgan stoops to see the screen. The devil—there he is.

She isn't holding onto the computer. It sits on her legs, tipping, unmoored. Gillian pushes its screen shut and re-holsters it in her bag. "Look, Morgan. If you want to make a visit to somewhere connected to Tricia, say a prayer, sing one of my old songs—something—I would be honoured to come along. I can easily get a Bible for you to hold or read or whatever, if it'd help you. You can even keep it after we're done. We could do that. Nothing's stopping us. And if you think it'll help…"

Morgan can't answer. Why hasn't Gillian fetched someone, some authority, folded the mess up in a sheet and delivered it to an expert, some keeper of a library of parchments full of medieval rules? Why isn't there a white man with a dark face who can give them Latin words to chant, beads to count, name an impossible artifact for them to go questing after—a strand of blue nylon from that tarp the police used to cover Tricia's body, the ear of one of the coyotes who tugged her bones apart, or maybe nothing but that Dante book still missing from the Edmonton Public Library system? Where is the ritual, the labour—the greater, stranger labour than going on, living from here?

14

Dean Orenchuk is bluffing. The moment he saw his move to gain leverage in negotiating an end to the Finnemore trial hadn't succeeded, he dismissed the notion of Tunnel Vision and began rooting for something new. He moves on, slightly disappointed, slightly surprised the family angle fell flat with the prosecutor. Someone told him that loopy church Joshua Lund goes to says he has to stop at nothing to put his family first. So much for that. Tomorrow, Orenchuk will close his case without alleging Tunnel Vision in the courtroom. No one will say a word about Paul Lund or his mental health or its influence on Joshua's prosecution of Brett Finnemore. Orenchuk knows all of this the moment Josh slams out of the courthouse briefing office. But he will not tell him until the morning.

Joshua Lund, on the other hand, is never bluffing. He stays at the office until midnight researching the law on Tunnel Vision defences. At nine o'clock, during another re-reading of *R. vs. Dix*, Gillian texts him from the street. She has brought food—a tray of grocery store sushi, she doesn't cook—and he needs to let her into the building so they can eat it before it gets warm enough to be toxic.

She sits on the edge of his desk while he eats—no chopsticks, just sticky fingertips—and takes a notebook from her bag as she listens to him ranting about Orenchuk's tactics.

"Passive aggressive?" Gillian says. "Orenchuk called you passive aggressive? No, no. You, Joshua, are full-on active aggressive."

He snorts.

She asks, "He can't really do this, can he? It's just some crazy fishing expedition, right?"

Josh wipes his mouth. "It's worse. It's attempted extortion. And he doesn't care if he can do it or not. Dean Orenchuk's genius is that he acts like he's never heard of the law. He just tries whatever he wants. He blusters away as if he believes what he's saying and it's all good law, and then he acts shocked and affronted by any objections. He tries everything, then waits to see if the court will put up with it or slap him down. He gets plenty of favourable rulings that way. It's disgusting."

"Sorry," Gillian says. She stands, pats Josh hard on the shoulder. "You know, there's nothing to it. Honestly— what Dana Randall said about Paulie and me causing a disturbance in the courthouse, it's nothing but deceit. But it is my fault she said it. I lipped her off in the courthouse a while ago. I didn't even have a good reason. I just let my stupid spite get the better of me and attacked her while she was standing around her workplace. It was downright nasty of me. And I'm sorry—sorry to both of you."

Josh lifts the nearest pen on his desk, taps it against an

open book. "Don't be like that, Gigi. It's not you. Dana and Mitch Randall are always happy to come after me whether anyone gives them an excuse for it or not."

Gillian slams the bottom of her paper cup against Josh's desk. "No, Josh, I did this. I didn't do it like the Randalls said—by throwing a fit at Paulie in the courthouse. But I did provoke them to pile on you this time. I did. Me."

"Why are you trying to own this? You don't have to."

"What? Why? Honestly, Josh, am I really so insignificant that I am powerless to make a mess of the business of someone like you?"

"That is not what I meant. Just," he tosses the empty plastic sushi tray into the trash, "just stop trying to get between me and this ridiculous legal issue a bunch of my grossest colleagues have cooked up. You don't have to intercede here—not for me. And that doesn't diminish you."

"Shut it, Josh."

"Fine."

She turns to face the wall of windows beside his desk, laughs. "All I really wanted to say when I came up here was that you were great in cross-exam today."

He exhales, smiles for the first time in hours. "Literary enough for ya?"

She is looking at him again. "Totally. You should start answering questions with 'to be sure' in your daily conversation from now on."

"Did I say that?"

"You did. Check the transcript."

193

He lays his forehead against the desktop. "I must be losing my mind. I don't have time for Orenchuk's Tunnel Vision nonsense. He knows that. I should be using this time to write my closing argument, like he probably is. It's a good thing I got a start on it already."

"You did?"

Josh lifts his head. "How could I keep from starting it? It's closing arguments. It's the best part. You want to read what I have so far?"

Gillian smirks. "A preview? Where's the drama in that? Closing arguments aren't just literature, they're performance art. It will says so in my dissertation. So, don't spoil it for me. Anyways, I can't stay long enough to be much help."

He lowers his head again. "I'll call Leanne and read it to her. She can't come hear it in person. There's some kind of mandatory Halloween carnival volunteer gulag going on at the kids' school this week. That's what I should really be doing tonight. I should be home cooking dinner while Leanne ties off goodie bags for four hundred school kids. I should be outside playing in big piles of smelly dead leaves with my own kids."

Gillian purses her lips. "They're okay. No really, I was just over at your place playing with the kids so Leanne could run one more 10K before the roads ice over. She's cool. The candy bags are done. Leanne knows being married to a good person comes at a cost—a luxury tax she has to pay in time served. Good people are rare. They need to be cut into pieces and shared. That's the price Leanne pays for

194

you. Bad guys, on the other hand—their wives get to keep them all to themselves. That's the price their wives pay."

The office is quiet. Josh looks across the wreck of his desk at his sister. This is the point where just about any married adult she knows would stop Gillian—abruptly or very gently—to add their further, wiser thoughts on marriage. Nothing she says about married life is allowed to stand as the final word. There is always more heaped upon or pared away from what she has observed, even when she is right. Josh is as guilty of doing it as anyone else. But tonight, he is only nodding at her over his marked-up copy of *R. vs. Dix*. "That's nice. Thanks."

When court re-convenes in the morning, Dean Orenchuk does not make a motion to have Joshua Lund removed as Crown counsel on the basis of Tunnel Vision. He has to do something to justify the delay he created in the proceedings so he re-calls Dr. Hale to testify one more time in a rebuttal that is actually just a reiteration of the points he raised during his own examination in-direct. It is improper but harmless, and Josh doesn't bother to object. By 10:30, the judge adjourns court for the rest of the morning. They will return for closing arguments in the afternoon. Josh has three hours to finish writing his. As the door closes behind the judge, he bolts up the aisle dividing the gallery, rushing out the doors of the courtroom.

Fine wisps of grey-brown hair over Sheila Turner's ears move in the breeze of his passing. "What was that? Was that panic?"

Morgan doesn't answer, doesn't look at her mother but tracks Joshua Lund's back as he passes. Is today the day Paul has shaved, cleaned up, clipped his hair, and come to be his brother? From behind, from outside the black pleats of the robes of the Court of Queen's Bench, there is no way to know.

Dean Orenchuk returns to the courtroom first at the end of the long break. He glances up from the pad of notes in front of him, as Josh and Coleen cross the bar, bowing.

Orenchuk lifts his chin. "Must be nice to get to deliver your closing argument without having to stand halfway across the room—no big gap between yourself and the jury."

Josh taps the back of his own chair, the one closest to the jury box. "We can trade seats until you're done your closing address. It's not a big deal. We can switch right now."

"No, no. This is the system. This is its preference. This is how the scales are tipped."

Josh answers only, "Warming up already."

Brett Finnemore is brought back to the courtroom. The judge follows and the trial reconvenes. Orenchuk does not want to be the first of the lawyers to make a closing address. It means he will not have the last word, but he called evidence in Finnemore's defence and now the rules of court compel him to be first. He complains about the unfairness of it out loud and on the record, before he begins his argument in earnest.

He reminds the jury of what the defence sees as the

highlight of Dr. Hale's testimony—the moment when he named Finnemore the most disturbed individual he had ever seen. "The Crown," Orenchuk says, "can't say for sure what mental state Brett Finnemore was in the moment Tricia Turner passed away. They have tried to call evidence that he was cold and rational, but I suggest to you it is just not there. What we do have for sure is Dr. Hale giving evidence showing Brett Finnemore was experiencing a 'psychiatric meltdown.' Remember that phrase? It's serious. A 'meltdown' is not a rational state of mind. 'Meltdown' is the same word they used to describe the Chernobyl nuclear accident that killed not one but thirty people, and made an entire city into a wasteland. That meltdown was destruction caused by a complicated and delicate set of circumstances that are the fault of no one person in particular. This meltdown is much the same as the one Mr. Finnemore suffered. His was on a smaller scale—only one person was harmed—but in the same way, the cause of it was a matter of tragic circumstances rather than any one sane person's fault.

"The truth is, no one knows for sure what Mr. Finnemore's state of mind was the night Tricia Turner died. I wasn't there, the Crown wasn't there, and none of you was there. But, the way our system works, the courts require someone to decide—and that is you. You are 'triers of fact.' Remember that phrase? It's serious too. That's our legal term for what you do. I'll tell you what it means. The judge will explain some strategies and rules for making your decision, and then you will go back to the jury room, close the door, and what happens next is up to you. This is a tremendous responsibility and trust. Only you stand between this young man—a man who suffers from a terrible, debilitating disease that could have stricken any of us or our children—and a powerful government out to make him pay for the effects of his illness with the rest of his life. All of this for a crime he doesn't even understand. Protect him from that faceless institutional revenge. That's why we have juries—to give the system a heart and a soul. Use that heart and soul, let it work on the tools the law has given you to find compassion, to find Brett Finnemore Not Criminally Responsible..."

A moment of quiet follows as Orenchuk takes his seat.

A reporter seated behind the Turners whispers to a colleague. "Good stuff. I don't know. The prosecution has really got his work cut out for him."

Gillian squeezes Morgan's hand. She is not sitting on the groom's side anymore. She is with the Turners, next to Morgan, their elbows linked. She is sneering at the reporter's comment, shaking her head, mouthing the words, "Not a chance." Morgan looks to see if Sheila has heard the whispering. She is sitting beside Morgan, chewing hard on a piece of peppermint gum. On the far side of Sheila, Tod sits motionless, not a creak from the bench beneath him. As the courtroom pause grows longer, Morgan is certain everyone must hear him breathing.

The judge speaks. "Whenever you're ready, Mr. Lund."

Josh springs out of his seat. "Members of the jury,

please bear in mind that the Crown is under no burden to prove Mr. Finnemore was suffering the acute effects of a mental disease. It is not up to the Crown to prove that Mr. Finnemore had the ability to understand what he was doing and that his actions were wrong when he killed Tricia Turner. That is the law. In Canada, everyone who admits to a set of facts like the one Mr. Finnemore and his defence have admitted in this case—anyone who admits to carrying out the kind of fatal violence Mr. Finnemore agrees he has inflicted on Ms. Turner—is presumed to have been able to understand what they were doing when they took that other person's life. That is the law. By asking you to find Mr. Finnemore Not Criminally Responsible for Ms. Turner's death, Mr. Orenchuk is asking you to make an exception—a perfectly legal exception—but one he must prove is warranted. It does not matter whether the Crown has convinced you Mr. Finnemore understood his actions. What matters is whether defence has convinced you Mr. Finnemore did *not* understand his actions. I continue to suggest to you that defence has failed to make that argument..."

What follows is a review of the evidence, witness by witness, thorough and painstaking. Finally, Josh approaches the end. "The most important evidence defence brought forward to convince you to find Mr. Finnemore Not Criminally Responsible is the testimony of an expert witness, Dr. Hale. You will recall Dr. Hale ended up agreeing that the Crown's theory was possible. It is possible that Mr. Finnemore might have experienced a psychotic break after, rather than before, killing Tricia

Turner. Dr. Hale was also unable to explain why Mr. Finnemore's antisocial personality disorder ought to be dismissed as a factor in his decision to kill Ms. Turner and defile her body. Dr. Hale was questioned at length about why he did not include any mention of Mr. Finnemore's antisocial personality disorder in his reports or testimony. I suggest to you that the answers he provided evaded the issue and failed to provide an explanation. I suggest to you he made a mistake, an oversight in forming an opinion about Mr. Finnemore's state of mind.

"As Dr. Hale testified, a psychotic disorder and a personality disorder are, quote, 'completely different.' He's right. With psychosis, people don't understand the world around them. With an antisocial personality disorder, people do understand the world. They just don't care about anything in it but themselves.

"With psychosis, like unmanaged schizophrenia, someone can rightfully call on the law to recognize their lack of understanding and protect them from inappropriate criminal consequences. However, with an antisocial personality disorder, the law offers no such provisions. Instead, the law steps in to administer criminal justice and to protect the innocent from further harm.

"I suggest to you that Mr. Finnemore's admissions of the facts of the case, combined with Dr. Hale's admissions under cross examination about Mr. Finnemore's mental state, expose profound weaknesses in the defence version of events.

"Other than this seriously flawed expert opinion,

what is left in the defence case for a finding of Not Criminally Responsible? Well, there's the report of a neighbour who passed Brett Finnemore in the foyer of Tricia Turner's apartment building during the same timeframe as the murder. He testified that Mr. Finnemore had a glassy-eyed look. 'Glassy-eyed'—what's a person supposed to look like right after killing his girlfriend? I suggest that this is not proof, or even good evidence, that Mr. Finnemore was disconnected from reality by a psychotic disorder during that time.

"Members of the jury, I suggest to you that defence has given you nothing—no grounds for stepping outside the normal course of the law. That normal course is to find Brett Finnemore guilty and criminally responsible for bludgeoning, dropping, and abandoning Tricia Turner far from her home and family. Brett Finnemore is responsible for all of that, and we ought to call that responsibility what it is: criminal."

It's finished.

Josh takes his seat. The gallery creaks like a ship at sea as the spectators shift along the wooden benches. The reporters seated behind the Turner family say nothing.

The judge pivots her chair toward the jury and explains the itinerary for tomorrow. They will reconvene in the morning, when she will give the jury instructions—a charge—and send them away to deliberate in secret. The twelve of them will gather their binders, go to a backroom where they will order lunch and remain sequestered, locked away themselves, until they have decided how to lock up Brett Finnemore.

14

There is still a world outside the courthouse and in it, it is
autumn, the shortest of seasons at this latitude, the time
when the old movie house on Whyte Avenue screens a
classic horror cinema revival. It opens with a mid-week,
midnight screening of *Nosferatu*—the bald vampire, possibly the first, possibly the strangest plagiarism of Stoker's
Dracula. It is a horror movie so old it's a silent film, with title
cards translated into English from German. Every image is
shot with a hand-cranked camera, a laborious human touch
running through it, marking the film like fingerprints.

For a long time, Morgan has known she needs to see
this movie. She has known it since she first saw a DVD
jacket for a remake of it in a rental store when she was
still a kid. Her parents never rented it. It is another movie
about a white-faced man in black—not hooded like the
Swedish *döden* or the INAC fire spectre, but similarly hairless above the eyebrows, posing in unlit doorways, negative black space framing his skull as if every dark thing
behind him were combining to form a hood. He is not
inside a house on a Reserve, or waiting on a rocky shore.
He doesn't come with sparking Christmas light wires,

no chess pieces, but with the histrionics of plagues and fangs.

The night the Finnemore jury is sequestered, deliberating a verdict for the man who killed Morgan's sister, is the night she will see the film. Morgan has never gone to a movie theatre alone. Not everyone knows this can be done. Morgan believes she needs a companion, and if she wants to watch *Nosferatu,* there is nothing to be done but to breach the manic loneliness of Paul Lund once again. As before, Morgan sits in her car outside her mother's house, sending him a text message in the dark.

There is no instant response, the way there was the first time she contacted him the night they went to the abattoir. The delay in his reply is not because Paul has not read her text. It arrives, sounding from his phone with a notification tone like a prayer bell at a Buddhist monastery. He slips his phone out of the pocket in the front of his hoodie barely far enough to read her name, "Turner," on the screen before tucking it away and attending to the task of signing a stack of papers for Gillian. Of course, the papers are not actually for Gillian, they are for Paul alone—applications to convince the government to acknowledge he is never going to be able to repay his student loans with his disability pension income and they ought to call off their collection agencies. The forms need to be in the mail this week or he will be billed another month of interest and penalties. In the blur of the Finnemore trial, Gillian nearly forgot to send them.

"You got a text," Gillian says when Paul's prayer bell sounds.

"Huh?"

"A text, I heard it. You just looked at it."

"Yeah."

There is a dew of sweat on Paul's upper lip. Gillian sees it and says, "It's not from me and it's not from Josh. Who's texting you at this time of day? Debt collectors? Or someone cool? Someone fun?"

He wipes his mouth against his arm, flips an application form to its front side, squinting at the fine print he has never tried to read before.

Gillian shoves his arm. "Why are you so weird about it? Is it a woman?"

Paul scoffs loudly into the application form held in both his hands. "They want me to write out my social insurance number again? Man, how am I supposed to—you remember my social insurance number, right Gigi?"

She recites nine numbers too quickly for him to jot them down. "The text is a girl."

"Gillian, give me some f-frickin' privacy."

She pulls the papers out of his hands. "Paulie, if you're seeing someone, you should let us know. It's not another one of those fake Russian Internet women trying to get money out of you, is it?"

"Oh, come on." He takes the forms back.

"Is it that lady upstairs? The one whose ferret tried to bite you? The one who tricked you into going with her to meet her dealer, in case he tried to pull anything?"

"Oh my gosh—" He has dropped the papers completely and stood up from the kitchen table.

She is following him, darting around shoes strewn through the hallway, moving toward the bathroom. "Paulie—Paul. Hey, you should let us know who you're seeing—"

He is calling from behind the locked bathroom door, over the racket of the ventilation fan. "There is nothing to know."

"—because dating can be dangerous. After drugs and alcohol, it's the most dangerous lifestyle factor Josh sees at work. It makes people act crazy. And—and you—I—"

The bathroom door opens. "Crazy—I'm crazy already."

"No, that's not what—"

He zigs past her in the hallway, back to the kitchen. "Will you please let me have some privacy, some dignity? I'm a grown man for—Are we done with the signatures yet? Where'd you put the envelopes? I think I've got some stamps here."

"Paulie, I don't want anyone to get hurt. You have to be careful, okay? People can be bad."

He picks up the papers and throws them back onto the tabletop, no stamps anywhere. The forms fan out in the air, his outrage fluttering onto the floor. "What—everyone is always telling me people are good. 'People are good, Paul, take your pills and stop freaking out. Stop worrying everyone is trying to hurt you, you weirdo. No one is talking about you. No one poisoned your drink. No one is at your window. No one wants to hurt you.' Everyone tells me that. You tell me that. You tell me people are good—children of God and stuff. But—"

"They are good." Gillian is yelling over his voice. "It's just that they're bad too. It's natural. People hurt each other all the time, mostly just by accident. You know that. What kind of wuss god would make children who don't have to power to be bad? How pointless would that be? Did you forget? You want me to quote scriptures? You want me to start with 'it must needs be that there is an opposition in all things...'"

"No. I know. Stop."

Gillian steps toward her brother, stands on top of the applications forms spread all over the floor. She clamps her hands above each of his elbows, shakes him barely enough to make him sway on his feet. "Everyone can be bad, Paulie—you, me, even frickin' Joshua."

He pulls his arms out of her hold. His force is swift and ballistic, propelling her away from him, twisting in a circle on the balls of her feet, like a movement in a dance. It is fast, unexpected, complicated by the paper under her feet. Crystals tumble through the tiny canals in Gillian's ears. She is spinning, without and within, falling into the toast crumbs and crushed cereal flakes of Paul's kitchen floor.

He howls. "Gigi! Oh my god—"

"Shh, don't—"

Paul crashes to his knees beside her on the floor. "I didn't mean to."

"I know. It's—stupid vertigo."

"No, it's me. It's me."

"Paulie," she calls over his voice. "Don't you cry.

Just look at me. This is the way things are—the way everything was made. Things are good but also broken and awful. Remember."

He sniffs hard against his tears, holding Gillian's elbow, nodding. He says, "I could maybe drive you to the hospital. We could try that. Or we could get a cab. Or—it's only a few blocks, I could piggy-back you to the emergency room. I'm stronger than I look."

She is breathing deeply, exhaling something between a laugh and a sigh, eyes closed as the dizziness slows, trailing into tinnitus.

"Please, Gigi. What do you need?" he asks.

She opens her eyes. "Patience—we need some patience. It won't last, it doesn't last."

His fingers sweat against her arm as he hoists her onto her feet, into a kitchen chair. "I'm so sorry."

"I know. Paulie," she says, "be careful. We need to be careful."

Paul watches Gillian over the top of his phone as he reads Morgan's text again. He does not believe his sister when she claims her equilibrium will drift back to normal on its own, and soon. Still, she won't let him try to drive her home himself, and calling Josh for help during a homicide trial is impossible. Gillian sits where Paul set her, on the gummy vinyl of one of his two kitchen chairs, her head resting on the stack of unopened mail he had brought for her inspection when she first arrived. They sit in the quiet mess as Gillian waits for her self to show up. Under her face, the papers and adhesives smell like a post office—like Christmas cards, grant applications, letters addressed to the magnificent Soeur Lund of the Canada Montreal Mission. She is coming back, plaiting together the faint traces of hope and happiness hidden in the fibres of the brown envelopes beneath her cheek. This is health—to find something to craft into a lifeline from whatever wreckage is left.

Paul pockets his phone as she rises to stand.

Morgan drives downtown, safely belted and locked inside Kang Shinwoo. Paul meets her outside, in the street, and she drives all of them across the bridge, finds a space to park in front of apartment buildings slightly less sketchy than Paul's own. From there, they walk to the avenue. Since the outing is hers, she offers to pay for his ticket to see *Nosferatu*.

"Hey, great," he says. "The fact is, I'm going to end up sleeping through most of it. Don't take it personally. It's the Zyprexa, not you or your movie that makes me sleepy."

They sit in the old theatre, shoulder to shoulder in the dark. Morgan has never watched an entire full-length silent film before. The picture is distant and dim. Scenes open and close, blackening in and out of the centre of the screen, like the dilating of a huge, slow iris. At times, the corners of the picture aren't lit at all. Everything is rimmed in dark shadows—arched doorways, kohl around the actors' eyes, paint on their mouths.

"There's a lot more smooching in this than I would've

expected for the olden days," Paul says, not whispering.

The male lead is comical, grinning headlong into danger and then hiding under a blanket to save his life, the escape strategy of a four-year-old child. Neither of them knows if it's supposed to be comic relief. Paul laughs anyway. When the hero recovers from a vampire-induced swoon and finds himself in the safety of the village inn where he was first warned about danger in the castle, he throws his arms around the landlady—a small woman draped in a shawl, no visible hair, face caked in movie make up. She teeters with his baby-boy force, rolls her eyes, pats his back.

Paul laughs in the dark—loud and opened mouthed. "Hey! Hey, did you see that? Our Gigi is in this movie."

The film cranks on, moving to a scene of sailors emptying a load of cursed dirt from inside a coffin onto their own feet. Swarm of rats rush out, biting a sailor through his shoe leather. He swings at them with the blunt side of a shovel and their bodies jerk and scatter, no stunts or effects, no rat body doubles, but real rigid onscreen death.

Paul groans. "No—No, there goes their 'no animals were harmed' declaration." He leans forward, covers his face, cups it between his hands, ready for tears. Morgan elbows him before he can get any sadder. It's a movie from 1922. It's like the Bible. All the rats, all the people, all dead from natural causes by now, no matter what.

He sits back in his seat, dries his palms against his pantlegs.

The story moves from the sea and the mountains back into urban Germany where the silly hero is reunited with his wife. "I figured it out," Paul begins, "His wife's look—I've figured out what's different about her. I'm pretty sure the actor playing her is a guy. Come on. Didn't they used to cast guys as girls all the time in the old days? Weren't they, like, forced to do it by society and stuff?"

He is thinking of Shakespearean theatre. This is German Expressionist cinema where every wife is a real lady. Morgan knows this thanks to Tricia—Tricia the former film studies major.

Paul huffs. "That doesn't explain how you know anything. My brother is a prosecutor. Doesn't mean I know the first thing about how to fulfill the conditions of my court order and keep from ending up with a criminal record."

Morgan looks to the screen where nothing is being shown but an unnamed extra lighting a gas street lamp in slow, real time. Tricia's education—her film studies career—it never meant much to Morgan when Tricia was alive. Frankly, it never meant much to Tricia, the girl who dropped out of school when her position as a receptionist was upgraded from relief to full-time with benefits. The keenness, the numinous quality of Morgan's memories of what she knows about her sister's life came after—when Tricia was dead. What Morgan remembers of her sister is heightened, carved out of the flat tableau of their history in high relief, every detail exaggerated, embellished by loss.

By contemporary standards, the movie is short. Paul talks through it consistently enough to keep himself awake until the end. He keeps Morgan there, talking after the theatre is cleared for its final cleaning. They go back to the avenue close to the time when the bars and clubs are shutting down. Neither of them notices until the Tim Horton's coffee shop they are sitting in fills up with the exposed skin and matted hair of reeking, yelling drunks. The dining room is small and dirty. Paul can hear what everyone else is saying. He needs to listen carefully.

The nearness of the other people in the café, the escalation of Paul's anxiety, it all keeps Morgan from telling him that tonight's rendition of her old horror story—the one about of the white-faced movie-man in black—is just like the others. The old horror movie makers created a monster without any sadness, not even for itself. Nosferatu, like the rest, is unknowing. Are monster movies nothing more than disaster movies—chronicles of natural phenomena unfolding with pestilence, feral beasts, wild fire, black cloaks descending on humankind inevitably, mindlessly, as if they're nothing but...

Nothing but NCR. Morgan exhales an unvoiced laugh.

Paul is openly eavesdropping on the couple at the table beside them as the woman rants about this month's unusually high Internet bill. His neck is craned away from Morgan.

Someone vomits on the floor.

They are outside again, looking for Kang Shinwoo in the dark, complaining about the movie's ending, where the only thing that can save everyone from the vampire plague is the hero's wife lying still and letting herself be bled to death.

Paul hums. "What would you rather have happened? You want her to lure the vampire into a tent, tuck him under a blanket, get him a drink of milk, and when he's nice and comfy—wham—hammer a big wooden tent peg through the side of his temple, right into the ground?"

Morgan stumbles where frost trapped thawing and freezing underground has heaved the concrete slabs of the sidewalk into a peak beneath her feet. She stops herself from falling, stands still on the sidewalk.

Paul stops too, closes his hand around the cuff of her coat sleeve. "Sorry, it's just another creepy Bible story. This woman named Jael versus an evil enemy of Zion, or something. I didn't make it up. It's a super old, bad ass lady story, like I thought we were looking for. That's all. Sorry, I—I didn't mean to bring up—anything—spiked—in the head."

Morgan is walking again. A tent peg through the head would have made a better ending for *Nosferatu*. Paul is right. Except for the part about the drink of milk. It's too strange.

He's laughing, letting go of her sleeve. "Sorry, the milk is canon, right out of the scriptures. We're stuck with it."

She is shaking her head.

"What gets me about your bald vampire movie," Paul goes on, "is that they spell it out, right on the cards telling the story, that we should never say the vampire's name aloud. What the heck kind of sense does that make when the name is the frickin' title? It's no good. The movie should be called something else, something safer like—I don't know—'The One-Man Apocalypse.'"

Morgan is still considering it when Paul blurts, "No good." He is animated all at once, vaulting ahead on the sidewalk, challenging no one in particular. "People need to stop using the word 'apocalypse' the wrong way. It doesn't mean the end of the world."

She jogs to catch up with him.

He's saying, "Sorry, it was me that brought the apocalypse into this. I did it. I hate that though. I hate how nobody knows what an 'apocalypse' is, anymore. It's a Bible word for uncovering something. Not the end, just a revelation."

Paul's pace slows to normal when a noise sounds from his coat pocket, the phony electronic prayer bell again. He doesn't answer it, but says, "If you want to get technical, it wasn't the lady's blood that killed the vampire anyways. It was the sunlight—plain old sunlight. It's so everywhere, so unavoidable—as normal as you can get."

Morgan stops on the sidewalk, not stumbling. Sunlight—it's perfect.

Paul is three steps ahead of her before he stops, looks up and down the street, looks again. "What's wrong? Who's there?"

Nothing is there. Everything is perfectly normal. Is he still sleepy?

"Not anymore. Not for hours and hours more to come."

She steps close, takes the front of his parka in both her

hands, folding the cold nylon between her fingers as if she has grabbed him by the lapels of a trench coat, as if she is a leading lady, a dame from another old film. She lifts her face for a high angle close-up. The street light has none of the tricks of the dame-taming soft lenses. Its effect is the opposite, deepening shadows beneath her eyes and nose—skeletizing. With this face, she tells him, "Come with me."

When Paul Lund listens to music, he sings along, always. His singing voice—the high, fine tenor—is alarming at first, not at all matched to the roughness of his outward appearance. Morgan has spent the last two hours driving alone with him in her car. She is settling into his voice, learning that it is beautiful. There is something excruciatingly, ironically earnest in a singing voice that sounds nothing like what we know the speaking voice of the same person to be. It's like an intimate exposure, a revelation. Is this an apocalypse? Is it happening here in her car as Paul Lund sings along to an old Psychedelic Furs CD he had in his backpack?

He sings a song about the ghosts we keep with us, and how they don't fade. Morgan has never known Tod or Tricia to listen to these songs or this band. It predates the Turner kids' musical sensibilities, falling into the gap between their music and their parents'. And though the lyrics of Paul's favourite song dwell on ghosts, though they're shadowy, they're not dark. The song is gentle and sweet, sung in a London accent, even in Paul's karaoke.

The singer of the Psychedelic Furs, he could be dead by now for all Morgan knows. If he is dead, Tricia might know him, wherever they are. Maybe he remembers, and sings songs about ghosts with a new, deathly smugness.

Morgan steers Kang Shinwoo westward, away from the normal, normal sun rising in the east. She wheels up an exit ramp, out of the furious southbound current of trucks and cars on Highway 2, turning toward the Rocky Mountains in the distance. Three years ago, she memorized the number of the range road she is looking for today. Once they leave the main highway, they reach it quickly. She turns the car again, onto a gravel road, tracking north.

Paul doesn't ask her if they are going in circles, if they are turning back already. He doesn't ask why they left the city when the Finnemore jury could come back with a verdict at any time. He sits singing, drumming the rhythm of the bass guitar line with one fingertip on the armrest of his door.

Morgan will never find the precise place. Of course not. No one—not her mother, not Tod, not the Victims' Services ladies, not anyone in the prosecutors' office—can tell her exactly where to go, and she doesn't have the police department's detailed topographical map studded with push-pins, or one of their blood-hungry search dogs. She can't sniff out her sister's first grave, here in these fields. Morgan stops the car blindly, along the dirt road, cutting the engine, cutting the music.

The interior of the car is quiet. It is dawn-light outside, blue. Everything is visible but nothing is very clear.

They open their doors, step onto the ground, and walk into a field of thick, brittle alfalfa stubble. Underfoot, it feels something like a bed of nails, like if Morgan was careful and meditative, she might be able to spread her weight over its mown tips and stand without bending them. That's how it feels right up until the straw nails snap into pieces beneath her feet.

Walking any further won't take her to the right spot so she stops, scans the dirt and cut hay. Behind her, Paul pulls his coat closed around himself, pivots in place to find the angle where the wind will blow his hair away from his face. He says, "I've never been out here before. It's peaceful, in a lonely, lonely way."

So near the foothills, the wind comes from the west—always the west—puffs the dust from the ground high enough for Morgan to taste it on the inner edge of her lip. She closes her mouth and swallows it away. Is this the rite—eating the dirt where Tricia used to lie? Do exorcisms have to be deliberate to have any power? In horror movies, they're about human will working on the darkness of an unseen world. Maybe in real life, they're about letting the brightness of an unseen world work its will on us.

Morgan begins, finally saying it as herself. The words are now her own. "Evil has entered this place, and it must be sent out."

Behind her, Paul speaks. "Evil has entered every place."

Morgan doesn't turn. She waits. Did Tricia stand waiting like this before she died? For how long? And when did she know? This place, the words, the everyday, everywhere evil—if Paul Lund is part of it, or even if he is just a monster, a natural disaster, Morgan will know in an instant. This is when and where. She will stand with her back to this man, a man with bottles of anti-psychotic drugs set on his kitchen counter like salt shakers. She will wait to be dragged into the dirt, choking on mouthfuls of it, fastened to the ground.

She waits, listening to the soles of Paul's boots breaking alfalfa stubble. He is close enough, thin and sickly but large enough to erase her from the view of anyone driving this obscure range road. From a near distance, he will look simply lost, alone, stringy dark hair tangling in the wind. He is rounding his posture, extending his arms, laying a hand on each of her shoulders.

"You okay?"

She turns her head to see his fingers on her shoulder, next to her throat and face. She says, "He left her here, somewhere—Finnemore."

A tremor moves through his hands. "Don't say it." Paul is not wrong. Finnemore's name is not the one to speak aloud in this place, at this time. If this rite has a name, it is not his.

Morgan opens her mouth again. "Tricia."

The pressure of the palms of Paul's hands against Morgan's shoulders grows stronger. There is no cinematic musical score, no ideal angle at which to see all of this, no lighting to tell her how or what to fear.

Paul's right hand tightens against her shoulder.

"Hey. Hey, don't hurt." He turns her face into his chest.

There is no hissing, no wailing, no stampede, no shadow rising out of the dirt to darken this field with its death thrall before dissipating into the air overhead. The music—Paul's voice singing old songs in Morgan's recent memory—it stays the same. Pressed against him, she blinks into the sunrise. It is tomorrow already, and she is so hungry.

16

Morgan and Paul are well without the Edmonton city limits when both of their phones sound at once.

"Where are you? The jury has a verdict and they're coming back in soon."

"Morgo, you're going to miss it. Court is back in any time now."

"Honest to God, Morgan, all I ever expected from you was to wake up and show your face this one day..."

"Paulie, I need you to tell me where you are and who you're with. This is important."

Morgan gapes at Paul across the front seat of her car in the parking lot of the roadside Humpty's restaurant where she has bought him breakfast. Sheila said it could take the jury days and days to decide on a verdict. Everyone said it. All the news people went home. Everyone went home.

Paul wipes at the sweat on his forehead. "No, no, no. I never said it. Josh's juries are never out for more than a day. I could have told you that. I knew that and I said nothing and I wrecked it. I wrecked this whole thing."

She is clattering the end of her seatbelt against its clasp. Paul watches the traffic through the rear window as she reverses. His phone sounds again, another text.

"This is serious, Paulie. Bring her back."

Kang Shinwoo does its best for Morgan, rocketing up the highway, between the livestock liners, the tankers, even the pickup trucks. It is too late in the year for road construction but too soon for blizzards so the roads are straight and fast all the way back to Edmonton. Morgan brakes hard at the southern edge of the city, dropping from a speed thirty kilometres an hour over the limit to just ten over it.

Paul is not singing but searching newsfeeds on the Internet.

Finnemore verdict—Tricia Turner homicide—chopstick murder—shopping cart murder—Brett Marshall Finnemore—Sheila Turner—Marc Turner—Joshua Lund—Not Criminally Responsible—slaughtered—

He is typing each term into her phone, ignoring the notifications from his own phone. He knows every one of them is a text from Gillian, every one of them stoking a feeling similar to the dread he knows so well—nearly but not quite the same. It's muddled with other people—not some abstract humanity he has to worry about saving or destroying, just a few people, hot and noisy with faces and voices. He knows this feeling. It might be guilt.

"Still nothing about a verdict in the news," he tells Morgan.

Inside the city, there is no easy path, no freeway from the northbound highway to the courthouse on the southwestern edge of the city's Chinatown. The distance grinds away, stoplight after stoplight. Morgan brakes and brakes, rocking into the steering wheel at every light.

"Morgan," Paul says. He is stony, his sweat cold as he stares through the windshield. "Morgan Turner. Switch places. Let me drive. I can drive. My meds give me an excuse, but really I just don't drive because—anxiety. This, though—this is an emergency. Josh and Gigi, everyone— I have to. All night long and I said nothing. This is my fault."

It makes no sense.

"Let me drive," he argues. "When we get to the courthouse, we won't want to waste any more time with parking and all that stupid stuff. If you're not in care and control of the vehicle you can just jump out and run inside. I'll wait. I'll circle the block as long as it takes. I have to."

At the end of the next block, stopped at another red light, they throw open their doors and dart around the hood of the car. They have stopped too close to the trailer hitch of the truck in front of them and Paul can't get out of her way. In the street, they grapple with each other until Paul leans across the hood and she climbs over his back, to the other side of the car. It's a spectacle. They are watched from the sidewalks, from car windows, bus stops, the high cabs of transport trucks. Everyone sees. Morgan can't hear them but she knows they must be negatively identifying her, nudging their seatmates saying, "Hey, isn't that the other Turner sister, the one who's not dead yet? What is she doing out here, playing in traffic with that skinny homeless guy while the verdict for her sister's killer is coming down?"

Paul works himself into the driver's seat. "Whoa," he says as he shifts the car into gear. His foot is pressed hard against the brake, a sharp crease folding into the top of his shoe. He curves both of his hands around the steering wheel before letting go, as if it's burned him.

Morgan shoves him with one hand.

"I'm going, I'm going. Yeah, I—it's actually been a long time—"

She shoves him again. If he can't do it, he needs to get out of the way.

"I can do it. I can. Okay."

They make the hairpin turn dropping them into the valley where bridges cross the river that splits the city into halves.

There is a new text from Sheila on Morgan's phone. "They've unlocked the doors. We'll be going back into the courtroom without you. Nicely done."

No one but officers of the court are allowed to use their cell phones inside the courtroom. Once everyone is seated, they will have no way to tell Morgan what's happening. Shut out, she will learn the verdict from the newscast on her car radio, at the top of the hour, after the traffic report and an ad for a discount diamond store. The road ahead is a steep hill rising away from the river into the tall buildings on the north side of its banks. The courthouse can't be more than seven or eight blocks away. Morgan might arrive faster if she got out of the traffic, ran to the courthouse on foot.

"No!" Paul says, turning into a new lane in a slow, perilous drift. "No, don't change anything now. It makes it worse."

They are on Jasper Avenue, at the very bottom of 97 Street, signaling left to close the final block to the courthouse. Morgan knows Paul will be too sick with nerves to attempt the turn until the oncoming lanes are completely clear all the way to where the road bends and he can't see any further. It won't do.

Morgan bursts out of the car. She hears him gasp before she slams the door and crosses the street between the traffic as it plods down the avenue. She runs along the sidewalks, the dirty paving stones. The stinging in her lungs makes her see sheet metal in her mind but she keeps running.

She is at the courthouse, up the concrete stairs, through the glass entry doors to the back of the security screening line. She steps right, left, and then cuts to the front.

"Please, please," she is saying to the guards. "Finnemore—he killed my sister and his jury just came back and they're all upstairs and I'm stupid and I'm stuck down here. Please—"

"Hey, sister, hey." It's a man with dirty hair and thick flannel jacket, no belt, the next person in line to walk through the metal detector. He is pointing to the space in front of himself, giving it away. "Here you go, right here."

On the third floor, at the back of a trial courtroom, a wooden door flies open. Morgan Turner is standing on the carpet, panting hard enough to seem like she is bowing to the bench. The room is as quiet as it ever is but for once, almost everyone inside it has turned to look at Morgan—the judge, the clerk behind her desk, the lawyers, reporters, Morgan's family, all of the jurors including the one standing on his feet inside the jury box. Everyone looks at her except for Finnemore himself. A hand reaches out of the gallery, from the groom's side, pulling Morgan into a seat. She doesn't have to look anymore to know it is Gillian Lund.

With the doors closed and all the disruptive civilians seated, the clerk clears her throat and addresses the man standing in the jury box, "Juror number six, on count number one, second degree murder, how do you find?"

The juror nods his head as he speaks. "Guilty."

"And on the second count, offering an indignity to a dead body, how do you find?"

"Guilty."

"Thank you, you may be seated. Juror number seven, please rise. On count number one, second degree murder..."

The jury is being polled, one by one, on their feet, out loud, speaking their verdicts as they are asked. Morgan leans forward in her seat, hands clamped on the back of the wooden bench in front of her. She has heard two guilty votes with no mention of Finnemore being Not Criminally Responsible for the murder. It's perfect—but how did the rest of the jurors vote—the ones she missed, the ones polled before she arrived?

Gillian's hand is on Morgan's shoulder, pulling her to

the back of the bench. She is stiff and won't move. Gillian leans forward, whispering, explaining, "It's a formality. The jury has to rule unanimously. One 'guilty' vote is the same as twelve. It's was all over from the very first 'guilty'."

Finnemore is guilty—no NCR status. He is not a patient, not a hapless monster but an abuser, a murderer, a killer.

"He did it." Gillian says, falling quiet as the rest of the jurors stand to repeat the guilty verdict.

Joshua Lund presses his shoulder blades into the back of his chair, rocking only very slightly as the judge accepts the verdict and thanks the jury. Dean Orenchuk glances at Finnemore, sitting blinking in the prisoner's dock. Sheila Turner nods between her earrings. Tod catches his own head in his hands.

The judge asks the jury if they would like to recommend a sentence. They are flustered, surprised—no one warned them this was coming. They nod and shrug at each other before the foreman answers, "No." Like everyone else, they want to go home.

The judge will hear the lawyers' sentencing submissions in the morning.

"Guilty," Gillian says when the judge leaves them all standing, free to speak out loud again. She hugs Morgan, squeezes her until it hurts both of them. "Guilty—he did it."

Of course he did it. Brett Finnemore never claimed he didn't do it. And then Morgan sees it, in Gillian's face

225

beaming across the room at her brother. "He did it."
Gillian was speaking of Josh. "He" is Joshua Lund. He
successfully fended off a Not Criminally Responsible defence more difficult than anyone here but Coleen and Gillian knows. He did it. Gillian has crossed the aisle, stands
at the bar, is reaching over it to shake Josh's hand with
both of her own.

At the back of the gallery, Morgan turns to her own
brother. Tod is gesturing with his head toward the empty
jury box. "You got all that, right Morgo? You got here in
time to hear it in the end?"

She nods. In the prisoner's dock, a sheriff has come
forward to fasten hand cuffs to Finnemore's wrists. He is
guilty, criminally responsible like they wanted. The door
behind the dock is open. Brett Finnemore is standing on
the tiles, the only patch of hard, uncarpeted ground in
the room, a surface the janitors can clean spit off of without having to bring a carpet shampooer. He is looking at
his own hands, raised at waist height in front of himself,
as the sheriff stoops to lock the chain between his feet.
Sheila Turner and her children say nothing to each other
as he is led away and the door is closed.

"Yes," Sheila says, "he's a criminal alright. But it means
we'll have to sit through a sentencing hearing, and your
father will get to read his idiotic Victim Impact Statement
in public. He'll probably release a copy to the press, set up
some interviews, iron the living hell out of a white shirt.
It's his big chance at a comeback. We'd better redo our
own statements. Where is that Coleen?"

"Mom, come on," Tod says. "No rewriting. Stand down and be a little bit satisfied it's turning out this way. This trial was a bloodbath. But it ended pretty good. Like, what other way would you want it to end?"

"I want," Sheila says, more loudly than Morgan has ever heard anyone speak inside this room, "I want it to end with Tricia coming back."

The chatter in the room abates for a moment. Tod backs away with it, retreating, jostling the reporter with the steno notebook standing behind him. "No. You don't even want it that way. You don't want anybody back. You and Dad—you both…"

Tod vents his breath, turns, extends one hand in front of himself, and pushes straight-armed through the courtroom doors. He will return to the house alone, cram most everything he has acquired in thirty years into his car, and drive to the Freibergs parking lot to sit browsing online apartment listings on the company Wi-Fi. The bedroom he leaves behind in Sheila's house will not be clean or even empty. There will be a dark grey film of lint on the carpet beneath the bed, crumpled black socks behind the door, a broken CD jewel case in the closet, and a poster he was handed for free at a hockey game rolled up and leaning against a wall. And on the floor beside his stripped bed, its reservoir still full of tepid water, Dreamweaver3000 will be left behind.

In the courtroom, the jostled reporter glides into Tod's empty space in front of Sheila. "Mrs. Turner—Ms. Turner, we're hoping to get an interview outside.

We're all set up on the southeast corner, the usual spot by the big sign, so the sooner the better."

Sheila shakes her head but reaches for the lipstick at the bottom of her purse, telling the reporters, "Yes, fine. Let's go."

The courtroom is clear enough for Morgan to stand uncrowded in its central aisle—not on the bride's side, not on the groom's. Tricia's horror movie has played to the end. The lights are on and the crowd is dispersing. The end of the roll of film is unanchored, a celluloid tag flipping against a reel still turning in circles. The movie is finished but not gone. It will stay with Morgan like every horror movie, still in her mind, projected onto her closed bedroom door, caught in the fibres of her pillowcase against her head like the smell of old smoke, plaited into the rugs on the floors.

Some families find better endings to stories like this one. Reverend Vreend's family—they must have made a better ending than this. Some families can agree to enter into détente between one another's states of grief, everybody joining in an armistice. When no one else in a family is willing to sign, this is how it ends.

It ends with Morgan Turner standing by herself in the eastern loading zone in front of the courthouse, waiting for Paul Lund to wheel around the corner in her car one last time. He comes into view, squinting and sweating, teeth bared, hazard lights flashing, half of the windows down, half of them up, windshield wipers screeching against dry glass, no music. He comes scaring swearing pedestrians and cyclists with the tight, unyielding angles he has been turning at all four corners of the courthouse block, not much of a circle to his circling.

In two nights and one morning, Paul Lund has freely offered everything he had to give to Morgan Turner. It is exquisite, and not nearly enough. He is not a devil but a hero—a doomed, suffering hero of a horror movie. It's a real movie, but one only he can see it. As he rolls toward her in her car—plastic hubcaps grating against the curb—Morgan already knows.

Paul thrusts the car into park. He is wrenching at the lever on the door, as if the car is filling with water, sinking. He spills himself onto the pavement, on his knees, clambering over the nose of the car, still drowning, gaining the sidewalk and grabbing at Morgan's hands and arms, pulling himself to standing against her body as she staggers with the weight and heat of him. Not enough herself—not yet—she will not be able to hold him for long. She widens her stance against their collapse, stumbling, stricken. His clothes are drenched, his arms around her back, a hand on the nape of her neck, his face pressed to the top of her head, hyperventilating her hair in and out of his mouth.

Dante's *Inferno*, the graphic novel version, has been returned to the public library. The book's call number on
the library website is the same as the one printed on the
first of Tricia Turner's posthumous overdue slips—the
one that arrived in the mailbox three months after she
died, when everything still meant everything to Morgan.
For years, she kept it. The day Morgan threw it away, she
checked the library's online catalogue against it one last
time before letting the slip go, and losing the power to
ever check again. The call numbers were the same as a
book now listed as "on the shelf". Does that mean it's the
same book—the same paper, ink, and glue? Was it slipped
back into a far-off branch's drop-box, maybe in the dark,
in the cold, by someone obscured by winter clothing
denser than any disguise? Or did the maximum security
Edmonton Institution find it among Brett Finnemore's
belongings while he was being checked into the penitentiary. A stolen library book must be contraband. It
couldn't stay there.

It is possible the library simply bought a new copy of
the book and reused the old number. Morgan won't ask

and she will never know. This is the ending she chooses—the one where the book in the library stacks is the very one Tricia held in her hands, carried through the streets, sent back somehow.

Inferno has been made into movies over and over again. One of the first movies ever made was based on the book. It's a silent movie, made in Italy in 1911, years before *Nosferatu* or any of the others. Morgan would like to watch all of it, more of it than she can find in uploaded Internet movie clips. She asked Gillian if she has ever seen it screened in Edmonton.

Gillian winced, told her, "No, I don't think anyone shows the whole of it anywhere anymore. Too controversial, too much potential for carnage and disaster."

It must be all the old-timey naked people in it.

Gillian laughed. "No hon, it's much worse. It's hate—the worst evil there is. Never mind it. Leave all of Hell and horror alone. Heck knows it's still there looking at us even when we stop looking at it."

This is how they spoke to each other, side by side in Gillian's car as she drove Morgan to the airport—the first and last favour Morgan ever asked of her. At the airport, Gillian Lund and Morgan Turner took their leave of each other. It was nothing like an airport parting in a Korean drama. No one was lying on the floor, crying. They stood face to face, and in one more act of friendship Morgan hadn't asked for, Gillian pressed one of her holy books into Morgan's hand. "It's not magic," she said. "Keep it anyway." Gillian returned to her brothers and her dissertation—the court transcripts, the found litera-ture stacked in boxes on the floor beside her desk at the university.

Morgan left Edmonton and came to China on an air-plane big as a small town, round and fat as a hog. She crossed the date-line high over the Arctic Ocean, in the space between Alaska and Russia where west stops being west. The plane cruised at an altitude where sunlight is so bright no one can bear to look out the windows for long and every shade is shut. When the clouds over the sea cleared away and the light softened, far eastern Rus-sia revealed itself, like the board of the Risk game Tod used to bully his sisters into playing on freezing Saturday mornings after The Fire Movie melted in the INAC pro-jector. Kamchatka, Irkutsk—not kitchen table fantasies anymore but roads and towns, fields and quarries, brown and green, ten kilometres below. Morgan cracked her window shade open, burned her eyes to see it for herself.

She ate citrus jelly candies Lilian sent with her in lieu of real tangerines which would have been a problem at customs. Lilian gave Morgan something else before she left: a new name, a Chinese name. After the matter was discussed in the Freibergs cafeteria for the better part of the day, Lilian and the rest of the staff agreed that Morgan Turner would live in China as 邱摩根. She practised writ-ing it on the only paper she had on the flight—the flyleaf of Gillian's book. Her Chinese handwriting is bad, and she is still too shy to show anyone. It will pass.

In Beijing, a shuttle from the English cram school

where she will be living and working waits outside the airport to take Morgan and two Australian men to a dormitory. For the first week, Morgan, the Australians, and the rest of the school's new staff will be tourists, staggering up high, uneven stone steps on the Great Wall, standing on the hot patios of the Forbidden City, in temples, tombs, and towers. People will take pictures of them without their permission, calling out "外国人"—foreigner—a word Morgan never thought to ask Lilian to teach her. She will learn it here. After the week of touring and jetlag, she will spend her days trying to explain the past tense to people who have always got along fine without it, showing them how to bite into their tongues, blowing out an exaggerated "th, th, th."

Beijing taxis are cheap, and Morgan has money in her bank account after letting her father resell poor rejected Kang Shinwoo on her behalf before she left Canada. On a night too hot to sleep inside her dormitory, she hires a car to venture alone outside the neighbourhood of her school for the first time. In a backseat with no seatbelts, she taps out the melody of a song playing in her head against the hard shell of the indestructible cell phone case Sheila gave her the day she flew away.

"For God's sake Morgan, you can't stay over there forever."

She thinks of Tod, learning the nuances of Freibergs's new, modernized hog scalding line, going home to his apartment, where his bed is an enormous reclining armchair, holding his body upright, his airway more or less open as he sleeps.

Leaning into the front seat, waving and pointing, saying "对对对" Morgan gets the taxi driver to let her out along the edge of the city's old moat. It is lined with parks—benches under willow trees kept safe by soldiers and policemen and old retired proletarians patrolling the streets with red arm bands and penchants for order. She is alone but not alone in a place where music plays and people gather to sing and dance and smoke cigarettes until the peace officers shut it all down so the rest of the city can get up for work in the morning. Morgan won't dance but perhaps she will join the people standing on footbridges over green water, tugging hard against kites—perhaps not.

She is not sure how to begin, here on the land mass on the opposite side of the planet from where everything else about her came to life. Summertime Beijing is hot and difficult. It is not an escape, not a transcendence, just a change, a revelation. This new quiet in the noisiest of places —with no language, no one—it will pass. The Chinese language will come along. She will sing it and sing it until someone starts to understand. People who will love her—they will come along too. It may take the rest of Morgan Turner's life to get hold of either of these, but at some time and in some place, they will come. She senses it in the mornings, in the Beijing sun—a perfect red disc burning through smog thick as a forest fire smoke. She rises toward it, into the rest of her story—out and away, passing into white sunlight, the well-lit cantos no one reads.

ACKNOWLEDGMENTS

This book was written with the support of the Canada Council for the Arts and with the help and inspiration of more people than I can name. It benefited from the University of Alberta's WRITE program where a chapter of it was workshopped by Thomas Wharton's senior creative writing seminar. Another portion of it was read by the school's then writer-in-residence Fred Stenson. Some of the novel's content has appeared in adapted forms in other publications, namely as the short story "Everybody's Horror Movie" in Fall 2016 *Prairie Fire*, and as part of the essay "Ice Cream with Superman and Kafka" in *Segullah* journal's 2017 *Seasons of Change* anthology. *He Comes Without Calling* is a real film and a masterpiece of childhood terror produced in 1975 by the Alberta Native Communications Society for Canada's Department of Indian and Northern Affairs. I first wrote about it for CBC Radio's *Definitely Not the Opera*'s "On Fire" episode in 2010.

As always, thanks go to Linda Leith, not only for her guidance and contributions as an editor and publisher but for her continued vision and guts—the flexibility of her interest in my stories as they and I shift and change.

Apart from writing colleagues, this book was nurtured by family, friends, and strangers. Certainly not least among these people are the victims of violent crime and their families, working through grief in view of ravenous news media and beneath the weight of a cumbersome, under-resourced justice system. Thanks go to personnel of that justice system for informing my research on everything from procedural details, to case law, to the jurisprudence of criminal prosecutions. If there are errors in any of the legal aspects of the story, they are mine alone. I must also acknowledge the influence of my sister-in-law, Stephanie Van Orman, who introduced me to East Asian popular culture as we raised our young children together, catalyzing a life-changing awakening in me.

And thanks to the men and boys coming in and out of the laundry room/office where I wrote this book, never saying anything about dinner. Of particular note are a fifteen-year-old son of mine who taught me the term "doctor's note crazy" and my sweet-talking husband who first described the smell of a hog barn as "the vomit of something fed on feces." I am truly blessed.

— Jennifer Quist